Cora Sandel was born in Norway in 1880 and died in Sweden in 1974. She is the author of the following collections of short stories: *En blå soffa* (*A Blue Sofa*), 1927; *Carmen Och Maja* (*Carmen and Maja*), 1932; *Tack dodtorn* (*Thank you, Doctor*), 1935; *Djur som jag känt* (*Animals I have known*), 1945; *Figurer på mörk botten* (*Figures Against a Dark Background*), 1949; *Vårt krångliga liv* (*Our Complicated Life*), 1963, and also of the following full-length works which have been translated into English: *Kranes Konditori* (1946) published by The Women's Press as *Krane's Café* in 1984; and the novels in the Alberta trilogy, published simultaneously by The Women's Press in 1980: *Alberta and Jacob, Alberta and Freedom* and *Alberta Alone*.

Cora Sandel
The Leech

Translated from the Norwegian
by Elizabeth Rokkan

The Women's Press

Published in Great Britain by
The Women's Press Limited
A member of the Namara Group
34 Great Sutton Street, London EC I V ODX

First published in English by Peter Owen Limited, London 1960
Original title *Kjøp Ikke Dondi*

Copyright © Gyldendal Norsk Forlag 1958
English translation copyright © Elizabeth Rokkan 1960

British Library Cataloguing in Publication Data

Sandel, Cora
The leech.
I. Title   II. Kjop ikke Dondi. *English*
839.8'2372[F]   PT8950.F2

ISBN 0–7043–5002–5
ISBN 0–7043–4005–4 Pbk

Reproduced, printed and bound in Great Britain by
Hazell Watson & Viney Limited,
Member of the BPCC Group,
Aylesbury, Bucks

I

"'Jazz instruments'," said Great-grandmamma in quotation marks. "'Battery' and so-called 'sax'. From morning till night. You see what it's going to be like."

"As long as it's new, Great-grandmamma," cried Lagerta loudly and far too brightly. "As long as it's new."

"You really mean that?"

"Yes, of course I do."

Great-grandmamma sighed. "You think I nag," she continued, "but what's an old woman to do? Look on and hold my tongue? For years I looked on and held my tongue, admit it Lagerta, I held my tongue. In any case you needn't shout as if I were deaf. I'm not deaf, not when there are only two of us. Why none of you can ever remember I don't know. Your roses are coming on nicely I see. Five buds on Caroline Testout."

"Yes, they're coming along." Lagerta looked up hopefully.

"But that's not what we were talking about," said Great-grandmamma. And with a small sigh, which might only have meant she was drawing breath, Lagerta bent over her darning again.

"That 'sax'—distress signals—caterwauling . . . "

"Not only that, Great-grandmamma. And we've all been beginners at one time or another."

"My dear girl, it's *supposed* to be dreadful," said Great-grandmamma vehemently. "Don't you understand? It's *supposed* to sound false and discordant, the way babies play when they get hold of something to play on. And they themselves are supposed to be primitive and vulgar and frightful. And then the kind of English they

5

bandy about, learned from second-rate films and second-rate records . . . "

The large living-room was filled with broad rays of sunshine. Light came from three sides through windows giving on to magnificent views of land and fjord and distant blue mountain tops. The veranda doors were open to the radiant North Norwegian summer: a summer which heaps light upon light, shining and brittle, only to fade too soon. It was fine with all the pleasant sounds of fine weather: hammering from the shipyard, children calling, the chugging of motor-boats. And somewhere a motor-cycle thundered by, and Great-grandmamma muttered: "Listen to that thing. They say there are two of them about now."

But like an abnormally insistent heartbeat, the thumping of jazz percussion could be heard in the depths of the house.

"If only they'd learn to read music," said Great-grandmamma as if to herself. "If only they'd learn so much as a scale on those instruments of theirs, but no, that's not necessary any more." She stood, her back a little bent, her hunched right shoulder turned towards the room, and inspected a rose bush, or appeared to be doing so. Lagerta never could tell exactly with Great-grandmamma.

She herself had sunk a little lower into her chair. Suddenly she clutched at her breast as if stabbed. A low mumble escaped her. At the same moment Great-grandmamma turned and caught the movement of arm and lips through her far-sighted spectacles. She was silent for a little before she said: "Are you in pain, Lagerta?"

"No, Great-grandmamma," said Lagerta, straightening herself.

" You caught at your breast?"

"It was just a movement."

6

"I wonder. Didn't you mumble something?"

"Did I?"

"Yes, you did, and now you look as if you'd been caught doing something wrong. And so you have."

"We all talk to ourselves a bit when we're getting on in years, don't we?"

"Rubbish. You're not in pain, but you have twinges. Atmospheric and nervous twinges. At my age that sort of thing puts you in a bad temper. But at your age— I'll wager you wake up in the night with them and don't get to sleep again. You've come to a pretty pass. You mumble, not because of old age—not yet—but for entirely different reasons. Mumbling at your age means you're ready to go to pieces. I suppose it was noisy here until the small hours? High heels tramping about, doors slamming—"

"No, Great-grandmamma."

" 'No, Great-grandmamma.' Don't call me Great-grandmamma all the time. I won't be Great-grand-mamma, not to youngsters like these. I'm a mother and a grandmother, and that'll do. They were scarcely born before you all started to say Great-grandmamma, and I let you do it, small and unknown to me as they were. But no sooner had they moved here than I realized I had nothing in common with them. I know it was noisy last night. It always is, and it's worse when Gregor's away. And here are you sitting indoors mending when for once we have a real summer's day. You could at least sit on the veranda or in the garden, but you daren't. You daren't, Lagerta, and things have come to a pretty pass for you. You ought to be over on the mountain or out in a boat on a day like this. We always were in my time, but you youngsters don't know what's what any more."

" 'You youngsters'—"Lagerta also spoke in quotation

marks and vainly tried a distracting little laugh. Great-grandmamma was unsmiling.

"I said you youngsters. I'm old, but you're not. Out with you into the fresh air and gather strength for something useful. Yes—I mean rebellion."

She stalked up and down the room, pinching her mouth so that it disappeared completely in her thin, flour-white little face. The tapping of her stick and her slight limp accorded to a nicety with the stubborn monotony of the percussion rhythm.

"Rebellion?" Lagerta made it sound inconceivable. "How does one rebel?"

"You know very well. Say no when no must be said. Put your foot down. Don't sit there mumbling."

"Putting one's foot down only leads to bickering."

"All right, then bicker."

"Bickering doesn't get you anywhere."

"Indeed it does. It can get you quite far."

"I don't believe in bickering," said Lagerta curtly.

"No, and that's why none of you will put an end to this situation. Among other reasons, that's why."

"Now I'll just mend this hole, and then I'll go out." Lagerta tried a new intonation and a new subject. "It's the children's socks," she said.

"So I see. Dondi isn't 'up to it', and Karine isn't superhuman. But those youngsters are big enough to mend their own socks. It would do them a lot of good."

"Oh, you know Dondi and her notions. And I can't let the children go about with holes."

"That would do them a lot of good too, to be made laughing stocks. And what's the hurry in this weather? Children anyhow go without them in summer nowadays. Sensibly enough."

"It may be rainy and cold tomorrow. We're so far north," said Lagerta patiently.

8

"Don't tell me how far north we are. But you Lagerta, *are* over-nervous, my dear. You must have something in your hands all the time. You can't rest any more, don't think I haven't noticed it. One can simply get too tired. Are the children in the cellar? It sounds like it."

"Yes, in the cellar."

"In holiday time, and on a day like this. Other young things are out in the fresh air. I saw a whole crowd of them with rucksacks waiting for the ferry. But these terrible youngsters—Yes, yes, I know, they're my so-called great-grandchildren. Even so, they're terrible."

Great-grandmamma halted and struck at the seat of a chair with her stick. "Playing jazz from morning till night on a summer's day," she said. "Here in the house. And in the cellar too!"

"They're in the cellar out of consideration for us."

"Consideration? Don't make me laugh."

"Is this one of your wicked days, Great-grandmamma?" Lagerta said it half jokingly, half unhappily, in the vain hope of really getting her to laugh.

But her expression did not alter. "One of my wicked days? I'm never anything else. It's a long time since I was in a good temper. It's nothing to joke about, Lagerta, on the contrary it's tragic. I too was a kind-hearted person once upon a time."

"And you still are," said Lagerta emphatically, with a hopeful and ambiguous smile.

"Nonsense. I'm wicked, old and wicked. Spiteful. Jonas will get like that too. We're normal, we react normally, he and I. You, on the other hand, get these twinges. We weren't as learned and well-read in my time as you are these days, but we knew it was dangerous to be too pious before it was put into books, although they tried to make us believe otherwise. I won't mention Gregor. He went out of his mind long ago."

9

"Now, Great-grandmamma—"

"Clean out of his mind. And now you're a little mad too. These instruments—how could you do anything so foolish, Lagerta? Didn't you think of Gregor? 'Jazz instruments' . . . "

"He asked for them himself," said Lagerta, playing her final, doubtful card. "The children came and thanked me so nicely."

"Oh indeed, and so you think they've turned into little angels. He asked for them himself, did you say?"

"He said: 'Let them have the things if you can afford it.' Children can plague the life out of you, you know."

"Children? Dondi, you mean."

" 'I shall have to spend more time at the cottage,' he said."

"At the cottage? I can see that happening."

Lagerta sighed openly, looking guilty and helpless, at a loss for anything else to say. She stuck her needle into a ball of wool, rolled up the sock she was darning, seemed to be tidying her sewing basket a little, and then just sat doing nothing.

Great-grandmamma paced up and down, silent too for a time, as if she had fired her last shot. Then the notes of a piano suddenly mingled with the jazz rhythm. She halted, looked up at the ceiling, and said vehemently: "The piano! The piano as well. Beethoven if I am not mistaken. Mixed up with all this jazz."

"You can't hear the jazz upstairs, Great-grandmamma."

"Can't hear it? When the whole house is shaking? She should be down at her 'business' at this time of day, at her 'Beauty Parlour'. It's past eleven. It doesn't seem to be doing very well any more."

"These things vary with the times. Jonas says there's not much money about at the moment."

"When he wants to offer you some comfort, yes. There's

not much money about, but women want their hair to look nice, whatever the times. Kvale's door is never at a standstill, even though it's old-fashioned there and not smart. But you get your head clean and the curls last. Mr. Andersen can't manage everything I presume, however much of a lady-killer he may be. If it weren't for the fact that she has to have something to strum on at every odd moment, I suppose the piano would have ended up in the cellar as well."

From above came a number of disconnected triads that had nothing to do with Beethoven, and Great-grand-mamma said, vexed: "Splashing about on the piano like that—I can't think of anything worse. But as long as Dondi doesn't gad about town in the car on fool's errands, you and Gregor are satisfied," she concluded, and started to pace the floor again.

"Satisfied? No. But we understand that life's not easy for her. She's from the south and—"

"What is there to understand? You're both afraid of her. Afraid. And why should it be easy for her? Are *you* from up here? Am *I*? We came from the south too once upon a time, and sometimes *we* thought it was pretty far north I imagine. Those who can't hold out must go. As for travelling—since the war, none of us has had the chance to travel as much as she has. But the one person who always turns up again is Dondi. I've hoped more than once that—"

"It's easy to talk, Great-grandmamma," broke in Lagerta. "When one is married and has children—"

"Married and has children! Dondi isn't married, nor has she children. That's not what it's like to be married and have children. Yes, go on, laugh. I'm used to nobody understanding what I mean."

"Gregor loves her," said Lagerta firmly.

"Oh yes, yes."

All of a sudden the piano switched violently to Grieg and then fell silent. First the left hand gave up, then the right faded away despondently in the middle of a bar, livened up again with a couple of small, stray broken chords, and stopped. Great-grandmamma gave a dry little laugh. "Might have known it. 'Get something out of music' indeed. It had to be a grand piano of course; an ordinary piano wouldn't do. But that was your fault again, Lagerta, it always is. Several thousand kroner out of the bank. And down the drain."

"That was for the sake of the children too. We had no musical instrument in the house. We may still get some pleasure from it."

"When a grand piano has stood there for five or six years with no more than a few odd bars being played with the loud pedal full on, it will never be used for anything else," asserted Great-grandmamma emphatically. "If there's one thing I hate it's slovenly pedalling. Messing around with music I call it. As for the children, it was right to buy them a piano. Yes, I'm wicked, a wicked old woman."

"We're all of us a bit wicked these days," said Lagerta, wearily. "This overcrowding doesn't improve things, and . . . "

"And Dondi," interrupted Great-grandmamma. "From first to last Dondi. We could have put up with overcrowding and a lot of other things if it had't been for Dondi. Because we're made that way, and she isn't. And as for overcrowding? There's been a war, and devastation, and occupation, everyone's overcrowded. Who isn't?"

Great-grandmamma stopped in front of Lagerta, paused for effect and thumped triumphantly with her stick. "Dondi isn't. Three large rooms and a kitchen, four counting the maid's room in the attic. A living-room like this, better than this where the view is concerned. Do you

12

call that overcrowding? In these times? Help with just about everything, food handed in at the door all ready cooked, while you live down here with Karine and have to sleep on a sofa in the dining-room."

"They have two big children. A boy and a girl can't share."

"They're still not overcrowded, not as things are these days."

Lagerta bent her head, accustomed to Great-grand-mamma's attacks, powerless to answer them, but stead-fast in her attitudes and actions; patient, prepared to be outdone, but tired. She made no attempt to reply, she had replied too often. She affected to tidy the sewing basket again.

"And now jazz instruments," persisted Great-grand-mamma mercilessly. "Gregor asked you for them, you said? A poor, irresponsible person like Gregor. You should have more sense, Lagerta."

"When Gregor's at home it's understood that the children play at the Eilertsens," said Lagerta, rather sharply this time. "And they have their school."

"The school? They're the despair of their teachers. They only just escaped being kept down a class this year. Is this an understanding with Dondi?"

"With Dondi and Gregor."

"Indeed. I can't make out how you afford it all. Does that money of yours breed? Money doesn't usually these days."

"I don't spend much myself, and Jonas is clever with money."

"He must be clever with yours then. With investments abroad. There are currency restrictions all over the place, but still . . . Well, I don't understand these matters. I'm only too glad none of mine's invested in anything, and that I have my modest little annuity. That was Øyen's idea, he stuck to what was safe. Things look rather quiet down at Jonas's these days."

"Business seems to be quiet everywhere at the moment."

"I suppose so," said Great-grandmamma resignedly. Tired, her mind drifted. She tied the ribbons of the enormous straw hat that had come from Paris in its time and had not really been designed for a chin strap; arranged the lace cuffs on her light grey dress which had been altered many times, but still kept a hint of easy summer elegance; sighed, made as if to go, and said:

"Gregor is still at the cottage, then?"

"He only went up there a few days ago, Great-grand-mamma."

"I was only asking. Sometimes he returns home quite quickly."

"He'll get more peace up there in the future. The children will sometimes be practising here too."

"So that's what you and Gregor have worked out between you?" Great-grandmamma was in full harness again and thumped with her stick, incensed.

"We haven't worked anything out."

"No, what would be the use? What can be worked out in this house? Except that now you'll have that terrible girl Kaia from the chemist's running in and out again."

"Dondi thinks she ought to look after her."

"You needn't shout, Lagerta. You make me so tired with your shouting. Look after Kaia? They don't need anyone to look after them, neither she nor Dondi. They browbeat everybody, both of them. Gregor threw her downstairs last year; he turned aggressive for once, soft soul that he is. But he's hardly out of the house before—"

"I can't throw her downstairs."

"No, there are some things you can't do. You're too

14

good for this world, as the saying goes. I thought to myself the first time I saw you: too good for this world. You came all that long way, young as you were, and that was all right as far as it went. But that you should have stayed, year in and year out—After Dondi joined the household too."

"Do you want to get rid of me, Great-grandmamma?"

"Yes and no. I want you to have a different life from the one you lead here. It's high time."

"I lead the kind of life I like."

"Rubbish."

"It's no good talking to me. By the time Dondi came I suppose I had put down roots here."

"Yes, and then you thought her 'pathetic'."

"I wasn't the only one."

"Maybe, maybe, the first few days, but not longer. Do you remember that cameo of hers? A high-necked black dress and a cameo. Smooth hair in a coil at the nape of her neck. Thin, pale, quiet, modest. Handsome, goodness gracious yes, handsome. Piously enthusiastic about Gregor's books. I remember I thought, she's putting too much into the part, she's exaggerating. They'll see she's acting, Gregor and the others. I was the only one to notice.

"No, when anybody 'pathetic' seizes control the game's up," said Great-grandmamma in a different tone of voice. "Things can only go from bad to worse. She didn't act at all badly. She exaggerated, but not badly. She understood her part all right. She acts well to this day, fairly reasonably too when she wants to, and that's when you have to be particularly on your guard. Dondi has a large repertoire."

"Oh yes," escaped from Lagerta.

"So you think so too?"

"Think what, Great-grandmamma?"

15

"That Dondi has a large repertoire?"

"I didn't mean it quite like that. I was thinking of something else."

"I see. Well, I'll be off. I've scolded enough for today." She made a helpless gesture with her stick, as if hitting out at something quite futile, and started towards the door. Lagerta got up to see her out. But Great-grandmamma halted in the middle of the room and turned abruptly. Her blue eyes, keen as an old sailor's behind her spectacles, looked straight into Lagerta's. "Do you never want —long—to be rid of the lot of us? To be rid of those you love most? To vanish into the world with a stranger? To shed all responsibility?"

"Heavens, what questions," said Lagerta, caught off her guard. "At my age?" she said, and attempted a small laugh again.

"At your age, at your age. The years are passing, Lagerta, soon you'll be old."

"I am old."

"Nonsense. Not too old, not for anything," persisted Great-grandmamma, disregarding Lagerta's shake of the head and indulgent smile. "Today you do look wretched, but you're handsome for your age, really handsome. You look well-dressed too, though your suit is shiny at the elbows and the seat."

"I've had it since before the occupation."

"I know that. Everything we have dates from before the occupation. But you wear it as though it were new, you have the art. Still, today you might have put on your summer dress. Why didn't you?"

"I don't know, Great-grandmamma."

"Oh, it's like that is it?" Great-grandmamma took a few steps towards the door and halted again. "I don't like people to throw away their lives," she said. "I don't like them to sacrifice themselves."

"I don't sacrifice myself."

"What *are* you doing then? Here you are with twinges, stabs in the heart, talking to yourself. Not because of old age, not yet. Because of pent-up anxiety."

"Sacrificing oneself must be distressing and difficult, surely, but nothing here seems distressing or difficult to me," Lagerta interrupted in a calm, matter-of-fact, if a little too high-pitched, tone of voice.

"I've told you, don't shout. Distressing or difficult? If Dondi isn't distressing and difficult, then I don't know what is. Your nerves are at breaking-point, Lagerta. And you could be living far away—further south—abroad—"

"When they take their music away it'll be all right, Great-grandmamma. It does bother me a bit too."

"It's far more than the music, my girl. You're at your wits' end, let me tell you. And if you believe they're going to take their music out of the house . . . "

"Gregor will insist."

"Gregor, poor henpecked Gregor? If only it could lead to his living at the cottage for good, and refusing to answer the telephone. But he daren't do that either. No, Lagerta, this business of giving in to Dondi's whims— goodness gracious, the whole performance—"

Great-grandmamma looked up at the ceiling again.

A high-pitched feminine voice could be heard from upstairs through the open veranda doors. It spoke quickly, without a pause. It was impossible to distinguish the words, but the voice held its own against the thumping jazz. Lagerta's face, which had just relaxed again after Great-grandmamma's last outburst, aged with exhaustion. "I do hope she's not phoning Gregor. He must have a little peace."

" 'A little peace'? As if a little peace could help him! A great deal of peace, peace for good, is the only thing

17

that might save him. It was probably too late ages ago, but—"

The door opened quietly. It was Karine, reddened with steam, her head bound up in a scarf. She dried her hands on her apron and announced: "Master Jonas is coming to lunch. He's sent up vegetables from the coast steamer and veal from Ryan the butcher. Didn't give me a chance to tell him I was in the middle of the wash with Edwina here helping and that we were going to have porridge. Well, I suppose we'll manage. Edwina will have to carry on by herself for a bit . . . Proper madhouse here today, that's what it is—heaven knows what Edwina thinks. You can't hear yourself speak in the cellar."

"Thank you, Karine. It's a phase, Karine," called out Lagerta at the closing door.

It opened again, and Karine pronounced: "Yes, leading to something worse, something far worse."

The door closed for good. Lagerta sighed. Without stopping to think she said: "You must stay to lunch then, Great-grandmamma. Sit in the sun in the garden until it's ready."

"Isn't that just what I've been saying? You're too good for this world. Fancy inviting me, angry, disagreeable old woman that I am, though it's not Christmas or Easter, nor even an ordinary Sunday. You enjoy the veal and the vegetables, you and Jonas. I'm glad he's coming up, it will do you good. You know I don't like eating out. Besides—to sit in the garden on a day like this, with all the doors open upstairs and down—no thank you."

"Next time we have something nice then. You're not out when you're here with us surely?"

"At my age that's out. And as long as I have my good hot-plate, and as long as we have some electricity for a change . . . Now don't let Dondi and those dreadful children of hers eat it all up for you. Well, as I was saying—"

"What were you saying, Great-grandmamma?"

"As I was saying, now I've been here. It has to be done, I was brought up to it, and upbringing sticks. I'm glad every time I manage to get away without running into my so-called great-grandchildren. They always madden me. But I wish I could stop saying what I think; I only upset you. Goodness gracious, Lagerta, why don't you get really angry for once—with me and Dondi, and the whole kettle of fish? We all of us treat you abominably, but the years go by, and you're still just as patient. If I could only put some fireworks into you . . . "

"What then, Great-grandmamma?"

"What then? I'll tell you what then. Then the catastrophe would come about. What you're afraid of and I'm waiting for. When you can't hold out any longer it will come. I'm beyond it all; it matters so little if I'm destroyed. For I am being destroyed. It was not always my nature to be angry. But the rest of you are being destroyed too. Even the sacred Gregor is being destroyed. His last 'collection' was an utter fiasco, the previous one —well, there you are. His private life has been a fiasco for years."

"Fiasco? The Swedish and Danish critics—"

"*Succès d'estime*. After all, he had 'promise' once. There you are, I've been hurtful again, and now I'm going. Keep your chin up, Lagerta. Be glad you haven't got me living here at any rate. If there's life in me to-morrow and the weather's just as fine I expect I shall look in."

"That will be nice, Great-grandmamma," said Lagerta bravely.

"My poor little Lagerta." Great-grandmamma patted her sympathetically on the shoulder, went towards the

19

door and again halted. "Have you seen the so-called great-grandchildren sitting in a circle arm in arm with their friends, swaying backwards and forwards like African savages in a trance? I have."

"Yes of course I've seen them."

"Have you heard Bella, when she sings in that hoarse and slow and—and lewd voice? Have you heard her sing: 'Keep on doing what you do to me, I love what you do to me'?"

"She doesn't know she's—lewd. She just imitates those records."

"Doesn't know? You're the naïvest creature, Lagerta. Did I call it singing? Nice sort of singing, I must say. More like shrieking. I won't say what kind of shrieking. Crowing, and bleating, and grunting. Surely it can't sound quite as bad as that abroad? Probably all the worst stuff reaches us here. It's the easiest to imitate too, they only have to bellow it. A phase leading to something worse: Karine is quite right. You surely can't believe these children will grow up into decent people?"

"Yes, of course. I'll come down the steps with you."

"Certainly not, I'm not a cripple. It's quiet in the cellar all of a sudden. Extraordinary. Down the steps, did you say?"

"They're so steep," said Lagerta.

"Steep? To the rest of you perhaps. Well, now I've done my duty for today, as far as I'm capable. Had my walk, had my walk twice, stood at the top of the hill and looked south, visited the churchyard, refrained from demonstrating. It's you who have come to grief, my poor Lagerta. That's what happens to patient souls. Condemned—"

"Condemned?"

"Condemned to be exploited by others, because they

20

can never shake off their terrible sense of guilt."

"Sense of guilt?"

"Sense of duty then. It comes to the same thing. Good-bye. Give my love to Jonas."

"I will. Good-bye Great-grandmamma."

Pale and unpleasantly disturbed by the words 'sense of guilt' and 'sense of duty,' Lagerta followed her as far as the door. There she sank down on the nearest chair, shut her eyes, muttered to herself, clutched at her breast, and then looked up again and met her own glance in the large mirror between two of the windows. There was her reflection, thrown into strong relief by the sunlight, and she suddenly hid her face in both hands and remained sitting thus, as if unable to bear the sight.

She looked up again when the telephone on the little table in the corner started to ring. She sat for a moment looking at it as one might look at something eternally recurring, at the stone which, no sooner pushed away, comes rolling back again. She pulled herself together, went across, and lifted the receiver. "Oh, is that you Dondi?"

The telephone droned. Perhaps only for a matter of minutes, but enough to drain the strength out of Lagerta, so that she shrank visibly from the handsome elderly woman with a good carriage and well-preserved figure into a tired, ageing shadow of herself. "But Dondi . . . ," she said. On droned the telephone. Back bent, eyes blank, Lagerta listened. "Dondi, my dear—" she said. "Wouldn't it be possible—" she said. "Can't I—" She got no further. The telephone chattered again.

"Yes, of course. No, of course not." Still no further. She looked round helplessly, found a chair, subsided into it. "Yes, I'm listening Dondi, I was only sitting down." Exhausted she moved the receiver over to her left hand. "I'm listening Dondi, I'm listening . . . "

Suddenly she raised her voice. "Gregor? But he's only just left, Dondi. For the sake of his work. We mustn't disturb *him* now. Why don't you come down, Dondi, and tell me what it is at least? If you won't tell me over the phone you can surely talk about it down here? Perhaps we can . . . What? He's coming? Have you phoned already? Dondi!" Lagerta's voice was despairing. She crumpled up completely and said no more, but sat abstractedly, her hand with the telephone receiver in her lap. The droning continued for a while, seeming to drain the last dregs of strength from her.

Eventually she let it go, but went on looking at it with set mouth. Until the receiver was slammed down at the other end of the line.

II

Jonas and Lagerta were having their coffee after lunch. Lagerta's beautiful, slim hands moved confidently among the objects on the tray, but the cup she handed Jonas shook a little. He glanced at it, then quickly over at her, drew in his lips as if stifling something he was about to say, stopped cleaning his pipe, put it down and took the cup. He sat stirring it, looking down.

The conversation had come to a standstill, as it sometimes did when they were together. Jonas took a sip of coffee, picked up his pipe again, got up, went over to one of the windows, and stood looking out while he set it going. The sun now shone on to the other side of the fjord, giving it a summer richness, with green reflections of meadows and hillsides deep in the sea, and glitter from the window panes of the few small farms. Its broad rays still shone into Lagerta's living-room, but through a couple of windows a little further along. It was the time of year when it sailed high above all the mountain peaks and nearly all the way round the room, except for a period towards early morning when it disappeared behind the north wall. But down over the town the shadow spread cold, the warmth was at an end.

Out in the hall the children could be heard shouting and yelling as they tore up and down stairs. Jonas blew out smoke and turned: "Are you quite well today, Lagerta? You seem a bit under the weather. You didn't eat anything either."

"Of course I did. It was delicious. And I'm perfectly well, just a little tired perhaps."

"Not surprising with these children in the house. I'll go at once and give them a talking to."

"Oh no, Jonas," came involuntarily from Lagerta. "They must be allowed to run about," she said.

"Run about?" said Jonas indignantly. But he sat down again, and now it was Lagerta's turn to steal a glance at him, as if disturbed by his acquiescence.

"Surely Gregor and I didn't make such a racket when we were boys?"

"You were past that age when I arrived, and Gregor was a quiet little boy. You were so different, both of you."

"They should be at table now," said Jonas, nettled. "Exceptionally good food too."

"They gobble their food, Jonas."

"Yes, and nobody teaches them table manners."

"I ought to have them all down here for meals, and try to make something pleasant out of it. It would be easier for Karine too."

"As if you haven't tried, but there were only scenes and recriminations. No, in this house it's better the less you all see of each other."

The conversation lapsed once more.

"It's American coffee, Jonas, not Liberian."

"I can tell that."

"I thought you hadn't noticed. I thought, after such a good meal . . . "

"Of course. And Karine hasn't forgotten the art during the war years. Excellent coffee. Thank you, Lagerta."

Silence.

Then Lagerta said, "It's so good of you to think of us up here."

"Good Lord, I almost live on the quay, I watch the cauliflowers and carrots coming ashore, so to speak." Jonas emptied his cup, stood up again, and walked up and down the room. It struck Lagerta, as it had so many times before, that he looked like a sailor, broad-shouldered, bronzed and weatherbeaten, with a tendency to sea legs, wherever he might have got those from, sitting as he did in his office all the time. Ought Jonas to be sitting in an office? But somebody had to, presumably.

Jonas halted, and looked straight at her with his grey eyes which appeared even lighter against the brown of his face than they really were. He said resolutely: "To be honest I had a purpose in coming today, but I didn't want to broach the subject while Karine was about, and I didn't want to—spoil our lunch with it."

"Oh dear, is it as bad as that?" Lagerta shrank a little. "Are you going to scold me, Jonas? Is it those unfortunate instruments again? Great-grandmamma has been scolding me about them all morning."

"I know. She called on me for once. She doesn't often come back to her old haunts. I've hardly ever seen her down there since Øyen's death. But she came today as she was concerned about the situation here."

"She made no attempt to hide it, as you can imagine. I got a lecture all right. Is that what you want to discuss?"

"No, it's not that."

24

"Surely the music shop hasn't sent the bill to you, Jonas? I told them expressly to send it to me."

"They haven't sent it to me yet. They'll try sending it to you first, I expect."

"Try?" said Lagerta, somewhat offended. "I'm the one to pay it, and I have the money."

"The money for that, yes. And a good thing too."

Lagerta stared angrily at Jonas. "I don't run up expenses I can't meet. And I don't mind telling you it worried Gregor very much that the children had set their hearts on those instruments. You know what children are."

"Yes, and Dondi. What Dondi wants generally comes about."

"Tell me what it is Jonas," said Lagerta, still with a trace of anger in her voice. It changed to a note of anxiety when she added: "Is it the children?"

"It's the usual thing," said Jonas. "Money."

"Oh, money."

"Did you expect anything else?"

"I don't know, I'm a bit jumpy these days. This modern *angst* you know. I sleep badly during the light nights too."

"What a lot of rubbish, you and your modern *angst*! And as for the light nights! You never used to sleep badly during the light nights."

"Oh yes, I did."

"Well, this racket in the house day and night can't improve matters."

"It isn't exactly sound-proof."

"It's damnable, that's what it is," said Jonas. He sat down, took up a book from the table and dropped it again with a slam.

"All villas are the same, Jonas."

"I mean everything, Lagerta. It must be brought to an end."

Lagerta made no reply to statements like that. She kept silent when faced with anything that could not be altered; it was part of her tactics. To gain time, Jonas returned to one of her earlier remarks.

"Money, you said, as if money meant nothing at all. Money can be embarrassing enough, when, for instance, you haven't any."

"What are you getting at now, Jonas?"

"I want to prevent you from further extravagance, if I can, because you can't afford it."

"Surely it's a matter of degree? I spend so little myself. I really do. And I don't know about being extravagant. It doesn't seem extravagant to me. What if I told you that—"

"That what?"

"Those instruments *had* to be found," said Lagerta with sudden determination.

" 'Had to be'?"

"They had to be. There's something you don't know, Jonas."

"And what's that?"

Lagerta sighed deeply. "The children were staying out at night," she said with an effort. "They were down on one of the wharves."

"Of course I know that," interrupted Jonas.

"You *know* about it?"

"I know they sometimes hung round an old gramophone on Eilertsen's wharf until the small hours. Those two and a number of others. They called it a club, a jazz club. People have heard the noise and watched them through cracks in the walls. The youngsters were playing the same records over and over again and listening to them as if in a trance. They danced, if you can call it dancing. They 'sang' too, of course. I don't think it was any worse than that, although people have hinted that it

26

was. This is a small town, remember. Of course complaints have been made to the school and to Eilertsen. I went down there a couple of times myself and threw the lot of them out. They were grey from lack of sleep, a shocking sight. But they weren't drunk, as people said. I've spoken seriously to Gregor several times. 'Take your children by the scruff of the neck,' I told him, 'or at any rate shut them in properly at night.' But poor, good-for-nothing Gregor—he's helpless to do anything with them. We all know that when he says no, Dondi says yes, 'as long as Father doesn't find out.' I've heard her myself. I believe Gregor called on the headmaster once to apologise and explain—But how did you get to hear about this?"

"You're not to call Gregor a good-for-nothing, he's not a good-for-nothing," exclaimed Lagerta indignantly. "I happened to find out about it one night some time ago," she continued more calmly. "The porch window was banging and I went out to shut it. I don't know why I stood there waiting. They came home in the small hours. And what a sight, Jonas! They both looked drunk to me. Their eyes were glassy. Bella's hair hung down as if it hadn't seen a comb for weeks. They were crooning their dance tunes, and those awful trousers she wears! All the girls wear trousers these days, but I don't know why Bella should look so much worse than the rest of them."

"Because she's Bella. Because Bella is a particularly insufferable child. Did they see you?"

"Yes. They seemed to come to their senses then, muttered something, and slunk upstairs. I didn't attempt to catechise them. But I spoke to Dondi the next day."

"She was the right person, of course. And then you got the whole rigmarole about complexes, I suppose? And the danger of not working out one's aggressions, and—"

"I couldn't pester Gregor," said Lagerta stubbornly. "And if Great-grandmamma had come to hear of it—"

"There'd have been a hullaballoo. You should have spoken to me."

"To you? In the first place they're not your children."

"No. If they were . . . " interrupted Jonas. "All the same you should have spoken to me."

"Gregor came to me the day after and asked me to get the children some instruments. He—"

"Yes, that's how Dondi gets what she wants," interrupted Jonas again.

"Well, at least they're not out at night any more, and we don't have to put up with the radio at all hours of the day."

"We'll see, we'll see. And is it any better to have a concert hall in the cellar? A jazz band and all the rest of it?"

Lagerta sighed. "I do so want to understand the children," she said. "I have honestly tried."

"Did you understand anything?"

Lagerta thought hard. "A few blues, something or other by Armstrong, the kind of jazz that has melody."

"Then would it be jazz?" said Jonas. "And as for Armstrong, that croaking raven!"

"I'm not just thinking of his singing. And he's not the only one who's hoarse. They're all hoarse, come to that. But there's something in their hoarseness, Jonas, something of negro sorrow, naturally, but something of the whole world's despair as well, of the feeling that you might just as well laugh as cry, since it won't make the slightest difference anyway."

Lagerta had raised her voice aggressively. Now she retreated from her unaccustomed position, muttering: "Well, I don't know of course. I know nothing about music."

Jonas looked at her thoughtfully. "I know even less. But never mind about the despair—which, it seems to me, can only get worse the longer they keep at it. The uproar on the wharf is surely part of this teenage craze that's sweeping the world at the moment, and which seems more pathetic and sordid the lower you go in small towns and limited circumstances. It ought to be stopped, but plenty of other things ought to be stopped. I had a visitor today. Andersen came and called on me."

"Andersen—?"

"Dondi's Andersen. The one who rattles his curling tongs down at her 'business'. There is only one Andersen, thank heaven. You helped to engage him."

"Oh, him. He's a strange person. What did he want?"

"Money."

"From you?"

"That was my impression. He was in difficulties, he said, and needed his money."

"What money, Jonas?"

"Money he's lent Dondi. Or 'invested in her business', as he puts it," said Jonas, who had put down his pipe, and was standing with his hands in his pockets, giving emphasis to what he was saying by nodding his head slightly in Lagerta's direction, as if to get her to see something obvious which she did not understand. He stressed the words as well, and then stopped himself. "I'm sorry, but Dondi does get on my nerves."

"Money he's lent her? But things have been going fairly well recently. It's a long time since Dondi was in difficulties."

"Oh, really?" said Jonas. "You are touching, Lagerta," he added affectionately.

Lagerta bent her head as if forced to submit to an insulting accusation. "How does that concern you?" she asked despondently.

"Not at all, you may feel. But Andersen evidently thinks it does."

"What did you say?"

"I referred him to his superior, Dondi. He laughed scornfully at the idea. That's exactly what he has been doing day after day for some time."

"Good heavens, Jonas—" Lagerta sat with her hands in her lap like a child caught doing wrong. "You didn't refer him to me then?" she said after a pause.

"No, I didn't."

Lagerta made no reply.

"But I do want to make sure you have the courage to stand firm when your turn comes."

"Andersen won't come to me."

"Andersen won't, no. It'll be Gregor. When it's something important it's always Gregor. He's not far off at the moment. Well, since Andersen came to me, I could take money out of the bank and pour it into the hungry maw of Dondi's business, whereupon the machine would splutter and run on for a short while."

"That's what I'd do, Jonas."

"But are you able to?" asked Jonas, as if talking to a sick person.

"I have been able to so far," said Lagerta hesitantly. "And Gregor never asks for money."

"No, he doesn't ask for it. He has a different method of approach, I know. You say you have been able to? Any reasonable person would say it's been a long time since you could."

"Reasonable? Are people always so reasonable? I believe in being a little unreasonable Jonas, I think it's necessary. How could we all get along otherwise?" said Lagerta, as if she had hit upon an unanswerable argument.

"How would unreasonable people get along, you mean? Well, to everyone his own luxury."

"Call it luxury if you like. People must have their luxuries. This one is mine."

"I wish I could fathom why you don't indulge in any other luxury," said Jonas, as if to himself. "Well, that's your own business. But if you get involved in this affair there'll be an end to your extravagance. For a long time at any rate."

"I'm already involved, surely? After all, it was I who—"

"Yes, I know. But I beg you not to get involved any further. I'm going to talk to Gregor, and before he goes up to Dondi too. I take it he's on his way home. When can we expect him, have you any idea?"

"Some time this evening. It depends on when he can get ferried across."

"Good." Jonas pinched his lips together and went back to the window. Lagerta, her face set and obstinate, looked up at his back. Jonas was going to be severe. This was nothing new, not during the past few years at least. He had been different as a boy, gentle towards his little brother. For the moment there was nothing for it but to keep silent.

She asked how much money was involved.

"Quite a few thousand. Twenty or thirty," came inexorably from the severe back. "—roughly calculated, and according to Mr. Andersen."

Lagerta was silent again. She was in fact struck dumb for a moment.

"He's supposed to have done without his wages for God knows how long. An odd situation, but there you are. They're supposed to have had some kind of an agreement, he and Dondi. His money was 'put into the business' as he called it, and he was to get interest on it. So he's been paying bills and meeting quite a lot of expenses, he says. And every time we heard there was something new down there it was Mr. Andersen who was behind it."

"Is that what he says?" Lagerta looked up. "But surely he must show—? Isn't written proof necessary? And signatures? And books?" Her tone was hesitant, implying that all this was mere conjecture.

"Bravo, not bad from you, Lagerta. Naturally he has to produce something better than mere assertion. He sat rustling a sheaf of papers with figures on them and wanted me to look them over. I told him to take the lot to Elveli, that it was a matter for a lawyer, and quite beyond me. Even you couldn't imagine anything like it. Some were receipted bills, but the rest—illiterate notes, scrawled in pencil on scraps of paper bags and God knows what else and signed—what *do* you think?"

Jonas turned to play his trump card. "Signed 'Dondi'. Just 'Dondi'."

"But are such things valid?" Lagerta was still hesitant.

"Bravo again, better and better. His wages were written on those scraps of paper, and he wouldn't get an *øre* of them from anybody else. But of course we're so respectable in our family. Idiot as he obviously is in other respects, he at least knows that. It was all a matter of drafts falling due, he said. And then he was going to get married. It didn't suit him to go to Elveli, he wanted the money on the spot. On the other hand, he wasn't able to plead any agreement about the length of time allowed for reimbursement. And that man was engaged to look after the accounts, because they gave Dondi migraine."

"To give perms and hair cuts too, Jonas."

"Quite so. The result is splendid. They've also been in trouble with the income tax authorities recently, he and Dondi. Their tax returns weren't accepted, but Dondi went up there and talked them round until they didn't know whether they were standing on their heads or their heels, and were only too glad to get rid of her. One of her usual weapons. Threats of tears into the bargain, and if there's one thing men fear like the plague . . . I must say it was considerate of the authorities not to bother you, Lagerta."

Lagerta had hidden her face in her hands. When she let them fall she seemed furrowed with exhaustion, as if after a long vigil. "I could tell there was something unusual," she muttered to herself. "Dondi's kept at home for several days, and . . .

"This morning she phoned me, in such a state," she went on, collecting herself. "I tried to calm her down, tried to make her leave Gregor in peace at the cottage. But no, he had to come home, he'd been sent for already. She wouldn't say anything to me over the telephone, nor would she come downstairs."

"Come downstairs I should think not! When was Dondi last down here? She uses the back door to avoid meeting you. Inexhaustible charity doesn't go unpunished."

"Charity!" Lagerta spat out the word.

"Call it what you like. You don't have two telephones in the house for nothing."

"We had to. Especially when Dondi started the business."

"You had to, or you'd have gone mad. Did you promise her anything when she phoned?"

"She didn't ask for anything. She was in tears. The only thing I managed to grasp was that Gregor was on his way home."

Jonas sighed. "If only he had the sense to stay at the cottage and let us deal with it all," he said. "What can Gregor do? Beg from you."

"I told you, Gregor never begs."

"No matter what you call it. There are many ways of doing it. You said yourself that he begged for those instruments."

"For the children, yes."

Jonas had something on the tip of his tongue, but kept quiet, and Lagerta remarked: "Poor Gregor."

"Yes indeed, poor Gregor," said Jonas icily.

"If there's anyone who doesn't complain—"

"I should hope he doesn't. You can't complain and then let things slide year in and year out. Not with any decency. A grown man who puts up with every mortal thing has no other choice but to hold his tongue. There she goes again."

The hysterical telephone voice could be heard overhead in a torrent of words. Jonas went over and shut the veranda door. "Damned nuisance in the middle of the summer, but I can't stand it."

He sat down. Both he and Lagerta remained sitting for a while, like condemned men when the fight has been hard and all hope is lost. They said nothing. Once Jonas glanced at Lagerta, but she looked away. She had by no means sided with him.

Pandemonium suddenly broke loose on the stairs, shouting, singing, clattering up and down. Jonas went over and jerked open the door into the hall. There stood Bella, making contortions in supposed imitation of a jazz singer, chewing gum with virtuosity while she gave out hoarse notes from deep down in her throat. Half way up the stairs Beppo was asserting something at the top of his voice. Neither of them saw Jonas at first.

"I've got the heebies, I mean the jeebies, I talk 'bout a dance, the heebie-jeebies," sang Bella in English. The gum shifted from one cheek to the other, her feet stepped out the rhythm on the floor, her body twisted, her hair tossed. The hysterical voice called down: "I won't see you, I'm ill."

A door slammed.

Beppo scrambled down again backwards, three steps at

a time.   Bella changed to a different rhythm and im-
provised: "Take care Mommy, take care, we know too
much, too much." Her brother caught hold of her arm in
warning, she noticed Jonas, and fell silent with a final
swing of an angular elbow, a final jerk of a long trousered
leg. As if in further provocation she manipulated her
chewing gum violently several times.

"Get out of here," ordered Jonas. "We can't have all
this noise."

"But we want the telephone," said Beppo defiantly,
also chewing, brazenly moving the gum about in his hard,
childish face. His lips alternately curled in a sneer and
relaxed in babyish uncertainty.

"Nonsense. Run out and telephone. It's not far to
town. It'll do you good."

"Can't we use Aunt Lagerta's phone?"

"No. Be off with you, Beppo. Out you go, Bella."

Muttering resentfully the children slunk away. "Even
the names of those children nauseate me," said Jonas. "All
this pseudo-romanticism of Dondi's. Bella and Beppo—as
if we were part of a circus."

He went over and threw the veranda door open again,
in need of air. "Memories of Italy—disgusting nonsense."

"It's not the children's fault, Jonas."

"No. It's not their fault they were born either. Dondi
was scarcely married before she wanted a child, she felt
so childless, as she put it. They were as poor as church
mice, living on their overdraft, but Dondi wanted a child.
The notion was human, she had her way. Tell me one
occasion on which Dondi hasn't had her way. She got her
child, two into the bargain. How like her."

Lagerta gave a resigned little laugh. "Well we can't
hold that against her, Jonas."

"We wouldn't either, if it weren't for all the rest of it,
if it weren't that everything becomes as damnable as it

35

can be when Dondi's involved. The children screamed like other infants, worse in fact. I was in Oslo and I heard them. They weren't very well looked after, I suppose. Gregor did most of it. Dondi spent her time at the Grand Hotel and the Theatre Café."

"Now you are being unjust, Jonas."

"A little, of course, as always when one dislikes a person. Not much, Lagerta, not much. Where was I—yes, then it would be so good for Gregor if they had a house of their own where he could isolate himself more easily. As you know, everything happens for Gregor's sake."

"It wasn't Dondi's fault they couldn't afford to keep on the house, Jonas."

"It was her fault Gregor invested his legacy in a house that they had to sell at a considerable loss, because Dondi couldn't live in a house at all when it came to the point. There was too much to do, she quarrelled with the neighbours, this, that and the other was wrong. They had nothing, they came north, we made room as best we could. This was a house too, but we had Karine. And you. Dondi had practically no domestic chores and was satisfied for a week or two. But Gregor had to clear out every time he wanted to get a few words down on paper. That led to a cottage, for him to work in. And then a car. Purely for Gregor's sake, so that he wouldn't have to be ferried to and from the cottage. As far as I've noticed, he has taken a boat each time. Then the war came."

"Gregor and Dondi both did their duty during the war, Jonas."

"Dondi did? Huh—well, never mind. She did move a radio once and we never heard the end of it. After the war—"

"The years since the war haven't been easy for anybody."

"Quite so. But everything possible was done for Dondi

in preference to anyone else. Dondi felt 'depressed' after the war. Dondi was unhappy up north, so Dondi travelled. Time and again. She went to this place in the mountains and that place on the coast. If it had made her well and happy I shouldn't have said a word, in spite of the fact that you were ruined by it. But did it? No. Dondi couldn't sleep, Dondi had migraine, Dondi took riding lessons. It was supposed to be good for insomnia and perhaps it is. That meant riding breeches, and boots, and a whip, and Lieutenant Evenstad. And Lieutenant Evenstad's horse. And rides—"

"It lasted for quite a time, Jonas."

"Yes, until Evenstad insisted that she take a fence. As he said, you can't let people out on horseback alone if they can't even clear a ditch. So Dondi gave it up. Evenstad told me about it himself. He was annoyed—said he didn't like to see an adult behaving like an infant. Dondi cried, of course. Or rather, screamed. She always screams."

"She hadn't the nerve for it, she's no sportswoman. Great-grandmamma really has set you against her today, Jonas."

"Andersen called on me today," said Jonas coolly. To which Lagerta had no reply.

"Sportswoman?" he resumed. "She managed to crawl up on skis to that ill-fated chalet where she first met Gregor. But never mind, she's no sportswoman. Still, I think it would have done her the world of good to have taken that fence. To have taken the consequences of one of her silly whims for once. A pity nobody forced her to do it."

"You can't use force on a grown person, not nowadays."

"I thought it was still used as a cure by determined doctors? It should be at any rate. It ought to be exhilarating to be forced to go through with something you fear without reason. A good, sensible therapy, it seems to me. But old Dr. Berven said as usual: 'Tut, tut, tut, we shall have to try something else, then.' And the riding equipment ended up in the attic. There it hangs as a symbol of our defeat."

"The defeat was mine, surely?"

"It was ours. If I had absolutely opposed it on that occasion and on others—The riding was by no means the worst."

Jonas stopped and took a deep breath, looking guilty and a little unhappy. He had talked himself into a passion, and said more than he had intended. "I don't mean to upset you," he said.

Lagerta, feeling somewhat superior for the same reason, smiled briefly and with some bitterness. "You came today to 'absolutely oppose' it then, Jonas?"

"I did."

Silence.

"You want to create a peaceful atmosphere for Gregor, don't you?" he said eventually.

"The advantage of all that travelling was that he got some peace," interrupted Lagerta, still feeling a little superior.

"Never for long enough. Surely work such as his requires a certain period of composure—a certain timelessness—before it can be begun? All that sort of thing is beyond me, of course. But if ever Gregor was able to achieve such composure, it never lasted long before Dondi was back again. He had the children too, and they got worse and worse. Tranquillity? Fat lot of tranquillity, I must say, although you looked after them as much as you could. Heavens, Gregor does write, he works hard when he gets the chance, but what does he produce? Every time Dondi went away I quietly hoped we'd seen the last of her. But she always turned up again. A little plucked and dishevelled, but otherwise unchanged. Never better, or pleased, as you and Gregor had hoped; always injured, always having quarrelled with somebody, always 'ill' for some reason, if anything more ill than before."

Beneath the veranda voices were raised in the lines of some popular song, indicating that there was certainly no question of unconditional surrender on the part of the children. The song grew fainter as they moved in the direction of the road. It was followed by a sombre solo overhead, the voice now fraught with tragedy and gloom. The garden gate banged.

In the weary silence that had fallen between Jonas and Lagerta a few phrases from upstairs could suddenly be heard quite clearly: " . . . terrible . . . they're killing me here . . . where *have* you been . . . I've phoned and phoned . . . "

They were submerged in the stream of words once more. "Kaia," said Jonas laconically. "Kaia can't be far away."

But Lagerta still felt superior. She had collected her wits and done some thinking.

"I'll see to this, Jonas," she said decisively. "This too. If I have to use my last øre."

Jonas looked at her for a moment as if she were a lost soul for whom there was little hope, but whom he would nevertheless attempt to save.

"And then?" he said mildly. "When you have seen to it, what then?"

Lagerta searched for words, and suddenly hung her head. Jonas drew up a chair towards her, sat down, and was about to put his hand on her knee, but thought better of it.

"Now listen to me, Lagerta, and let me speak my mind for once. There's nothing else for it, today we must speak

39

frankly to Gregor—and to each other. I don't think you can have evaded this thought either, Lagerta."

"What thought?"

"I don't think you can have failed to tell yourself that this work of genius for which we're all waiting will never see the light. The situation doesn't change, the pressure isn't relieved, Dondi will never be satisfied. We want peace for Gregor and there's only one way for Gregor to get peace. Can you remember anything besides trouble and discontent since Dondi came into the family?"

"Yes, I can," said Lagerta defiantly. She searched her memory for a moment, seizing on something at random. "Of course I can. I remember when they were here during their engagement, for instance. I had burnt my hand and it was bandaged up. So Dondi took my place at the head of the table and carved the joint. She was all in black, so slim, such lovely colouring, so smart. She had such a beautiful expression and I felt so fond of her. I thought: now I have a daughter—a daughter as well—"

"You're very charitable, Lagerta."

"I remember far more than that, Jonas. Let me think again."

"No," said Jonas. "I won't let you think again. That's how you commit follies. You're the victim of a misconception, you think you can curb Dondi. But nothing will curb Dondi. Gregor's salvation is to get rid of Dondi and the children as well. I know you think I'm harsh, but I'd suggest that we liquidate the business as best we can, sell the piano and the cottage and the car and—all right, don't jump out of your seat, we'll have to see about the cottage—and then club together towards a respectable divorce, so respectable that he won't be saddled with a guilty conscience. It will be expensive, but it can't be helped. And when I say 'suggest'—"

"You mean you're going to take advantage of the situ-

40

ation he's in? You're going to exert pressure on him? On someone like Gregor, so sensitive, so— your own brother, Jonas?" Lagerta's voice trembled with indignation. "He won't be able to write a word," she added triumphantly. "He won't agree to it either. He'll never leave Dondi."

"Won't he? Perhaps he has insensibly grown ripe for it? When patience such as Gregor's is exhausted, it is exhausted. As you know, it isn't the first time I've thought of this."

"I know," said Lagerta.

"As for curbing Dondi," resumed Jonas. "How many times have you 'thought again' and believed you were curbing Dondi? Just take the piano. One fine day it was suggested that Dondi wanted to 'do something with her music', so you bought a grand piano—during the worst period after the war, when we were having to pay reconstruction taxes and everything. It arrived by steamer and attracted no little attention under those conditions."

"It was an old second-hand piano, Jonas. And cheap at the price. I had the children in mind as well."

"The children indeed, who won't even learn to read music. Mr. Enoksen sent them home one fine day. As he said, he had better ways of spending his time than struggling with them. They just sat improvising on his piano and were impudent into the bargain, they laughed in his face. And a grand piano is a grand piano when all's said and done, your bank account was at a low ebb for a long time. You hadn't money for the smallest personal expenditure."

"Of course I had, Jonas."

"Your story was that there was nothing in the shops. I remember that bit of play-acting."

"It wasn't play-acting. There *was* nothing to be had. The tradespeople shut at midday for lack of things to sell."

"You could have gone to Oslo, to Stockholm, further afield. But no. Not even when the 'tide' came in again."

"There, Jonas, you see, the 'tide' did come in again."

"Would you for once like to know how it did?" Jonas halted in the middle of the room and looked at Lagerta as if on the point of committing himself to something decisive.

But Lagerta was not looking at him. She was looking downwards, her thoughts elsewhere, and she said wearily: "I rely on the fact that it did come in again, Jonas. You know how little I understand about all that sort of thing. I believe you implicitly."

"Then you'll have to try to believe me today too, when I tell you that all this must come to an end, and quickly, so that no one will have the chance to think it over."

He walked up and down in silence for a while. He, too, looked tired and worn. "All you do is sign on the dotted line," he said eventually. "You'll sign anything. Have you so much as read through one of your own tax returns? No, you haven't."

"But I know they're all right. I know nothing of mine could be in better hands than yours. I'm so thankful not to have to do it. My mind goes blank as soon as I set eyes on such papers. All the same, I manage Karine's bills all right," she added, straightening herself slightly.

"Well, they're simple enough, after all. And you trust Karine."

"Of course I do."

"So you can."

"Can't I trust you, then?"

"If I were you, I wouldn't put your trust in me quite so blindly."

"Don't talk nonsense, Jonas. Listen—when you talk about liquidation is that the same as bankruptcy?"

"In this case, yes."

"And you want to expose Gregor to that?"

"Heavens Lagerta, the word hasn't the same ring of scandal it used to have."

"It still means something that's gone wrong, presumably, it still means defeat?"

"Something that's gone wrong, and which you liquidate as honourably as you can, rather than leaving it to get worse. Am I to give a lecture on that as well?"

"No, thank you," said Lagerta abstractedly, lost in thought again. "I've known for a long time that Dondi's business wasn't a success," she said. "I didn't mind losing the money as long as it kept Dondi going. I was careful not to mention it, she would have taken it badly."

"Yes, indeed she would. But how long does anything keep Dondi going? Her music ended in strumming, her riding in foolery, her travels in foolery, and here we have the result of her becoming a businesswoman. An old hairdressing establishment which was never a success is suddenly put up for sale, and the two of you become demented. A 'modern' establishment was just what the town lacked. Here was the answer at last. Dondi would find her métier in life, the family flourish like the green bay tree, Gregor do without his advances. What a farce!"

Jonas halted again, and took a deep breath as if it cost him an effort to say: "The day Elveli called me up to find out what security you could offer, Lagerta, will always stand out for me as a day of dishonour. You weren't able to tell him yourself, you had referred him to me. *Without so much as breathing a word of it in advance.* Yes, now you look upset, and with good reason. It wasn't like you to go about things in that way, and not worthy of you either. I recognized another of Dondi's tricks, the *fait accompli*, and in my opinion it's one of the shabbiest. And you had sunk as low as that. You let her browbeat you, you degraded yourself. But of course I wasn't your guardian, I didn't say much. Still, it would have been reasonable if—"

"Yes, Jonas," said Lagerta. "I was a coward. It was wrong of me." She looked up, her eyes filled with tears. Jonas patted her on the shoulder: "Forgive me for being so impatient."

"Need we talk about this any more, Jonas?"

"I think we must. You need to see things in perspective."

"I do see them in perspective."

"That's just what you don't do," said Jonas. "Listen, she went off to Trondhjem to learn the trade. After a couple of months she was home again, because, she said, she couldn't wait any longer to get started. She wouldn't have been able to get the most insignificant job as the result of what she had learned, she wasn't even half-trained. Perhaps she might have been allowed to work as an apprentice."

"She has a bent for it, Jonas. And she's been through commercial school."

"Dondi has no bent for anything that demands regular, sustained effort. Commercial school!"

"She has a diploma."

"Yes, some document was waved around."

"It couldn't have been a fake."

"Everything to do with Dondi is fakery," declared Jonas. "You think she got a diploma, do you? If so, she flirted her way to it. No reasonable person would give Dondi a diploma for anything, only someone who had had his head turned. Mr. Andersen was called in more or less at once, as an expert in the trade and in business, an acquaintance from the hairdresser's in Trondhjem. And if it were not for the fact that you are respected in this town the combination would have proved impossible. You've acquired the reputation of being a mighty rich woman, Lagerta, and it's amazing what money will do."

Lagerta was lost in her own train of thought once more, as if adopting this device for her self-protection. "It's a pity about Dondi," she said. "She's so helpless really."

"Helpless?" Jonas laughed dryly. "If there's anyone in this house who isn't helpless, it's Dondi. Day after day she has a whole family waltzing to the tune she calls. I know some folk who are more helpless, at any rate," he added significantly.

"She's the kind of person who can never make anyone really fond of her," said Lagerta in her obstinate manner, quite unconcerned. "People like that *are* helpless."

"You think Gregor loves her, don't you?"

Lagerta did not reply, and Jonas said, "No, you don't think so any more."

"I don't know, Jonas, I don't know anything."

He stood and looked at her searchingly: "No, we don't know much. But I do know that's there's been something about Gregor during recent years—a certain easy-going acceptance of support which I can't stand. And nor can you. Neither of us like watching the deterioration of someone we're fond of."

"He probably doesn't know which way to turn," said Lagerta, distressed. "He's bothered by so many things, and—"

"He's getting pretty shabby, if you ask me."

"Shabby? But Jonas!"

"Is there any other word for it? He's sponged on you for years."

"What do you mean, sponged?" said Lagerta in anger. "Everything was a gift from me."

"It all depends how you look at it. And who turned him into a sponger? Dondi. How could he love her? He's afraid of her, as afraid of her as the rest of us are. More

45

afraid. And nothing degrades a person so much as fear. But to get back to the financial side of it—"

"Now don't mention securities and that kind of thing, Jonas. It's Greek to me and I'm incapable of listening to it. It's no good talking to me about all these remote, impersonal papers of mine that I've never set eyes on. It's just so much empty rustling. And as for figures—a look at them makes my head swim."

"The only advice I can give you is to learn a little Greek as soon as you can. I won't say anything about your securities today except that they're not bringing in much for the time being. And the little they are bringing in will stay where it is under present regulations."

"I know," said Lagerta patiently. "But every now and again my account increases, the 'tide' comes in again, just as it did in Øyen's day. A little less often perhaps. There you are, you see how stupid I am. Before you I had Øyen to help me all the time."

"You had Øyen, and for a long time you had no Dondi, and there had been no war for ages. The bank in Oslo and Øyen were able to be generous with a good conscience. It must have been pleasant for Øyen to play benign Providence, and you got used to having money in your pocket all the time."

"Dear old Øyen, he was kind."

"I've been kind as well. Much too kind. If only I could have foreseen all the surprises you were going to spring on me . . . No sooner had the tide come in, as you put it, than it ebbed again. And now we have to save the wreck of your property and the wreck of Gregor."

"But why didn't you tell me, Jonas?" Lagerta was following a short way behind Jonas's train of thought; she had difficulty in seeing the point, and arrived at it more slowly.

"Told you what?"

"That I had nothing left."

"I didn't say you had nothing left. I said that if you get involved in all this you'll soon find yourself empty-handed. And afterwards it may be a long time before the tide comes in again."

"You should have warned me earlier."

"I've been warning you all along. Though maybe I have my weaknesses too. I admit that I should have kept you informed, coldly, clearly and relentlessly, but if you think it's pleasant to speak one's mind in this house, you're very much mistaken. Feelings are hurt and offence is taken to right and left. You are broken-hearted, Gregor is injured, Dondi we won't mention, and Great-grand-mamma is angry—not with me, with the rest of you. Nobody opens his mouth here except under the direst necessity. But now it is a necessity, and you'll have to believe me without any figures or explanations. As for getting you to understand—you must forgive me, but I couldn't even attempt it. I'm going to look in at the office now, but I'll be back in good time. I must be here when Gregor arrives, so that I can talk to him before he goes upstairs. If not there'll be an uproar that'll beggar description."

"We shall probably have that in any case. As for talking to Gregor—what's the use? Does he ever talk to you?"

"Even less than he does to you. I presume he talks to you now and again?"

"No, Jonas, Gregor tells me nothing. I've never been taken into his confidence, nor have I tried to be. I remember too well what it's like to be young. Your nearest and dearest are the first you hide from."

"Well, he'll have to answer for himself today. We must have it out as to how this situation came about, and see to getting it on to another tack.

"I shall spare him as much as I can," added Jonas

quickly. "I don't intend to make things any worse for him. Now you rest while I'm gone, Lagerta. The house is quiet for once in a while, and if Kaia comes—"

"It will be even quieter. There's nothing so ghastly as the quietness after Kaia has been here. I shan't be able to rest, it's impossible."

"Huh," said Jonas. He made an abrupt, awkward little gesture, as if to put his arm around her, opened his mouth a couple of times as if trying to say something. Nothing came of it. Lagerta did not notice. She had hidden her face in her hands.

Jonas left her. As he opened the door into the hall, Kaia from the chemist's came in through the front entrance. She and Jonas greeted each other in the manner of adversaries, as briefly and distantly as possible. Kaia wandered upstairs. Jonas slammed the front door behind him, locking it as he did so.

Lagerta wandered about the living-room, baffled and irresolute, taking up a piece of sewing and putting it down, picking up her darning and rolling it up, removing a leaf from a vase of flowers, searching for a book in the bookshelf, sitting with it a moment and finding that she was not taking any of it in, walking a few paces from window to window and finding herself looking at nothing, repeatedly talking to herself. Now and again she started at the sound of voices above which would suddenly rise and as suddenly sink to a murmur again and die away.

She caught herself repeating meaningless, incoherent phrases. "My fault," she was saying. "My fault—"

"Can't act differently," she said, as if defending herself.

And now and again she would say: "Only what I deserve," and "Just what I deserve," with the emphasis on 'just', hanging her head in shame.

III

"Mrs. Styrsvold, who can that be, Karine?" Lagerta looked up anxiously from the book with which she had finally settled, not one word of which she was taking in. Here was Karine announcing a completely unknown visitor at, to put it mildly, an inconvenient time late in the afternoon, as if Lagerta felt calm enough to talk to strangers now.

"She's—she's Mrs. Styrsvold. She lets out rooms and she has a little café—down on Strand Street, next door to Eidem's place. She's divorced from that fellow Styrsvold. He's away in the Arctic now."

Quite clearly none of this was any recommendation to Karine: "I said Madam was resting, it wasn't convenient today, I said. But I couldn't get rid of her. It was important business, she said, 'pressing', and 'urgent'."

Lagerta was already on her feet. Her thoughts whirled in her head: a small café—the children have done something wrong at the café, broken a window, behaved atrociously, ruined the gramophone, it's happened before. Best to get it over with.

She drew a pocket comb through her hair, brushed down her skirt and straightened it. Small measures, not of much use, but instinctive among women, emergency expedients at the last moment. This had been the kind of day when small attention is paid to one's appearance.

"Ask her to come in."

Lagerta covered her face with her hands for a second as if to cool it, to tauten it up, and then looked composedly towards the door. Mrs. Styrsvold seemed to take in everything at a glance as she entered, handsome and capable, in the prime of life, confident and well-dressed. "My name is Mrs. Styrsvold," she said. "I took the liberty—"

Now she was looking directly into Lagerta's eyes, and Lagerta saw that Mrs. Styrsvold's were blue and very beautiful and completely fearless.

"Won't you sit down, Mrs. Styrsvold."

As she sat down herself, Lagerta caught a confused glimpse of someone in a hurry turning out of the garden gate. Who could it have been? From the back it looked like Karine, but Karine had her hands full and never goes down to town without being dressed up, wearing a hat, and walking with dignity. The person at the gate had her head tied up in a scarf, and a large apron, was drying her hands on the apron, and almost running.

A feeling of danger crept over Lagerta. It *was* Karine, Karine looking just as she always does on a washing-day afternoon. What is going on?

"Is there anything I can—?" she managed to ask, looking as resolutely as she could into the blue eyes observing her so calmly.

"That's what we'll have to find out," interrupted Mrs. Styrsvold, placing a determined hand in a smart glove on the edge of the table. "I could have gone to our Jonas, but—"

She noticed the dismay in Lagerta's face and added in explanation: "Yes, I said Jonas. Everyone here in town says Jonas, they always have. People like our Jonas, but they say he's in difficulties. You're supposed to be rich, though."

The gramophone at least, thought Lagerta. Radiogram probably. That'll be expensive.

"Rich? I'm afraid I'm not exactly rich."

"Well, that's as may be. Perhaps nobody is rich any more, but that's what people say, and everyone wants what belongs to him. So I've come about settling these debts, about the money that belongs to my fiancé,

Andersen. Because, you see, we've made up our minds to get married."

"Really?" said Lagerta hesitantly. "How nice. May I congratulate you?"

"Thank you. We think it's nice too. He's made up his mind now, as I said, and our Dondi can think what she likes."

"My niece engaged Mr. Andersen to do the permanent waving and the accounts," said Lagerta sharply, now as stiff as a ramrod. "I'll thank you not to—"

Mrs. Styrsvold interrupted her eagerly: "Yes, and our Dondi was supposed to wash their heads and do the manicures. But when she wasn't out driving the car her own head ached so much that—It was really grievous that head of hers all the time. And as for the manicures—"

"My niece is not strong," said Lagerta. "And are you on intimate terms with her, Mrs. Styrsvold?"

"Not strong, is she? A pity we're not all as strong as she is. No, I can't say I'm intimate with her, but everyone calls her Dondi, you know. Gregor's Dondi, as they say. But you're probably in the dark about a lot of things. As I was saying, we want to get married, Andersen and I."

"There's surely nothing to stop you doing so?" said Lagerta, still icy, but remembering at the same time that she had heard something about Andersen's marriage plans earlier that day. They suddenly took on a disquieting aspect. She lost a little of her cold confidence.

"What's stopping us is that we want our money, all of it. We're going to set up house. Of course, I have my own home, but everyone wants a few new things when they get married, don't they? And if we're to get anything out of the business we shall have to expand as well."

"Are you referring to my niece's business?"

"We can call it that if you like." Mrs. Styrsvold laughed a little. She looked at Lagerta almost with liking, and certainly with sympathy. "We can call it that for the time being."

Lagerta attempted to collect her thoughts as best she could. Business matters are beyond me, she said to herself, I'm afraid I'm bound to say something silly. She heard Mrs. Styrsvold saying: "Andersen has tried to phone Dondi—I mean your niece—time after time for days on end, but what's the use? She had that migraine of hers, she was in bed with an ice-pack on her head, she was too ill to hold the receiver, she was going to be sick. Every day she was just as bad. She's tumbled to it that there's something wrong, for she's stayed at home for nearly a week now. But she doesn't understand what a bank draft is, or she pretends she doesn't. We knew that, but Andersen wanted to proceed correctly, as he said, as long as she's responsible. Today she said Gregor had been sent for, as if that would help. Gregor can't do anything one way or the other. And now it's urgent, it's urgent, as I said."

"I can't understand how Mr. Andersen could have let himself be persuaded to lend so much money," ventured Lagerta cautiously. "Surely he must have been aware of how matters stood for a long time, and—"

"Men!" interrupted Mrs. Styrsvold. "Are they aware of anything when they're in that condition? But I suppose you're in the dark about that too. News always comes last to those who are nearest. And you've never married, so I expect you're above all that sort of thing."

"I don't think I quite understand what you're talking about," said Lagerta, again as stiff as a ramrod, and understanding only too well. A subconscious, unformulated anxiety was suddenly given substance, an uncomfortable chill gradually enveloped her.

"I'm talking about Dondi, about your niece. She makes them so wild, you wouldn't believe. For when they think they're getting somewhere at last, she screams, does Dondi, screams so people can hear her right down the street."

Lagerta made no comment, and Mrs. Styrsvold continued undisturbed: "Kaia from the chemist's is a cut above Don—above your niece. At least Kaia's natural. She goes out with that doctor of hers, it's true, she's gone with a good many, but she's not the only one, and she is natural. It's hard on the chemist, he's a fine man. He was a simple soul to marry her, but these menfolk are simple. Andersen was simple too, to think something might come of it between him and—and your niece. I told him so from the beginning, it won't come to anything, Andersen, I said. She's not superior, he said, she's 'common', as he put it—he's from the south you know. She's like one of us, he said. She's married one of the high-ups, I said. They can have things as democratic as they like nowadays, on the coast steamer and all over the place, and where she came from I don't know, but she married one of the high-ups, and you'll be made to feel it soon enough. And he was. She screamed and screamed, and scratched him too. People came running in from Settem's and from the street outside, they thought it was murder. Andersen is a good fellow, he made them leave without any fuss, though goodness knows what sort of an explanation he made up. But after that he'd had enough of it, he came straight to me and he said: You know, Johanna, I think it had better be us two after all, if your inclination's not changed, for with you there's never any nonsense. If you get in the mood you put up with the consequences, a man knows where he is with you. And that's true enough. You can say a lot of things about me, but I will say I'm straightforward in that respect. Dondi—pardon me, your

53

niece—went about smiling and stroking herself up against him as soon as they were alone. And her voice went all peculiar, as he said. She had a divan standing there too, in the back room, all ready for use, as it were. To lie down on when she had migraine, so it was said, but Andersen seems to have got a different impression. He got it when she lay about complaining and asking for compresses for her forehead—and wanting her hand held. So when they had gone on like this for some time, and he had put in his money too—well, I suppose he thought he could expect something in return. Perhaps he thought she was the kind that likes to be taken with a bit of force, some people are like that, you know. Personally I think she's a fool in that as in most things— she doesn't know what she wants. No, it's best to be straightforward in all matters in this world, and we should be able to expect it of each other."

"You must be very straightforward, I'm sure, Mrs. Styrsvold," said Lagerta, hearing her own voice, cold and neutral, with amazement.

"Yes, I think I can say I *am*," said Mrs. Styrsvold. She nodded her head twice with emphasis and looked Lagerta straight in the eye: "And, as I said, Andersen has come to his senses."

"To his senses?" In an undertone Lagerta tested the word as if it had a strange taste.

"Yes, he sees that nothing will come of it. He won't get the business that way, nor will he get—your niece. I can't tell you the number of times I told him so, but when menfolk go off the rails they're just crazy. Now he's going to take it over himself, as I said."

"But can he do that?" Lagerta asked more for the sake of asking and in order to get a little breathing space, than be informed about Andersen. Much of what Mrs.

Styrsvold had said she had probably missed, but the certainty of something vaguely sensed and feared remained with her, chilling and unpleasant.

"If I add my bit he can. And he can when he gets hold of his money, all his money. We shall have to see whether there'll be anything left over for Don—for your niece. We're honest folk, and you people up here have done your best, everybody in town says so."

"Everybody in town?"

"Yes, everybody. But I expect you're above that as well. And quite right," declared Mrs. Styrsvold firmly.

"Quite right too," she went on, warming to her subject. "All the sympathy is on your side. And Andersen's clever, as long as he can get away from Don—from your niece and her tomfoolery. *Lazy,* that's what she is. Maybe she should have had a different husband, not Gregor. People who write—"

"Keep him out of it, if you please," said Lagerta in the same cold, neutral tone of voice, hearing as if in a dream the sound of a car beneath the windows. It swung round on the gravel and stopped, the door slammed, it drove off again. A car from town at this time of day?

But when there came a quiet little knock at the door as if someone was in a hurry and would prefer not to be noticed, but wanted to warn the company of his arrival all the same, she knew at once who it was. The door opened, and there was Jonas.

Mrs. Styrsvold, sitting with her back to it, noticed nothing and went on with what she was saying: "I don't mean to run down Gregor, he's a nice man, but there can't be much go in him, the way he lets his wife lead him by the nose. After all, Andersen's not the only one Dondi has flirted with, there are others. When we had the Germans here there were plenty who gossiped about her, but everyone knew of course that you were all right, and our Jonas and our Gregor and the old lady. Dondi knows best herself how far she went, but most people considered she was too friendly, she smiled at them and she winked at them, and once they say she was sent flowers, but it seems she didn't accept them, didn't dare to I shouldn't wonder."

In the background Jonas shifted and coughed, and only then did Lagerta feel really relieved that he had come.

But Mrs. Styrsvold calmly turned round, looked at him coolly and smiled a little: "Well, it's quite an art to pass through closed doors."

"Which I cannot master. I knocked in the ordinary way," said Jonas drily, coming closer.

"What is all this, Jonas? Do you know anything about it?" Lagerta looked up at him in bewilderment.

Before he could say anything, Mrs. Styrsvold replied: "Our Jonas? A bachelor living in the middle of town and he wouldn't know anything about it? He'd have to be mighty simple."

"You are evidently intimate with the whole family, Mrs. Styrsvold," said Jonas as drily as before.

"I may come from the islands," said Mrs. Styrsvold, equally drily, "but I came here as a child, and I've heard people say Jonas and Gregor and Lagerta as long as I can remember. It's a childhood habit, and if anybody wants to say Johanna to me, I have no objection."

"Thank you, I think Mrs. Styrsvold will do, especially in purely business discussions. I suggest we transfer the remainder of these negotiations to my office. You can find me there whenever it suits you from tomorrow onwards. My—my aunt is not very well acquainted with the matter. She holds joint ownership, it's true, but she has never taken any direct part in the business. I'm sure you will authorize me to negotiate on your behalf, Lagerta.

As I have said, I am at your disposal, Madam, but today—"

"The matter has to be settled today," said Mrs. Styrsvold energetically. "We have large payments due the day after tomorrow, in the morning. Andersen has got himself in a fine pickle, he's been far too kind and patient. I've told him time and again, you must clear all this up, I said. And now I'm putting my foot down. I'll marry him all right, but I'm not going to pay out all that money. Andersen has been to Jonas once already today, without any result. We've been phoning and phoning Dondi—your niece—for a long time. And now we want to get the whole thing settled quickly, we think we have the right to insist, and that it would be best for you people up here too. So that not too much of the story gets about. I came up here today because it's my belief that this is where the money sits. But if Jonas is authorized . . . "

"I have acted as my aunt's business agent for many years, ever since old Øyen died. I am thoroughly conversant with her affairs."

"And I'm conversant with ours. Just as thoroughly, and more so than Andersen. I remember old Øyen well, although I was only a child. He was a fine man, everyone said so. Can we go down to your office at once?"

For a moment Jonas looked undecided. Then he said: "Very well, let's do that."

Mrs. Styrsvold faced Lagerta resolutely. "I really do feel bad about this, and I'm sorry. But things couldn't have gone on much longer as they were. And especially now that Andersen's made up his mind. You have to take men up on what they say, that's my experience."

Lagerta said nothing. She bent her head stiffly in farewell.

"If I might be allowed to say what I think," continued

Mrs. Styrsvold, "you're too *refined* for this sort of thing. Much too refined. It's a crying shame that you should be mixed up in it. But you're too kind-hearted, we've thought so for a long time in this town. And a bit innocent, as people are when they've never been married or anything. We'll try to settle it as well as we can, so that you suffer as little as possible. Nobody denies that you're a fine, straightforward person. And you were in good faith, I'm convinced of that now."

"Thank you, Mrs. Styrsvold," said Lagerta deprecatingly, fervently wishing the conversation would come to an end. Jonas held the door open: "If you would like to come with me now, Mrs. Styrsvold, I am at your disposal. But I'd like to remind you that my time is short and that it's late in the afternoon."

He followed her out, and turning in the doorway, gave Lagerta a look of mingled apology, encouragement, sympathy, and entreaty.

Lagerta collapsed on to the nearest chair and sat paralysed, her mind a blank.

Not for long. A bell-pull jangled suddenly through the house and continued for some time; it sounded violent and desperate. She pressed her hand against her pounding heart. It wasn't the doorbell, it came from inside, from upstairs. An unusual and by no means harmless undertaking in itself. And on a day when Karine has the washing to do, and has been to town into the bargain, and . . .

Lagerta peeped anxiously round her own door.

Karine was on her way upstairs, her tread ostentatiously heavy, her back disapproving. She walked across the floor above, and then out again. Other footsteps on high heels followed hers. A couple of short sentences were exchanged, sharp as rifle shots. And then Karine's voice on the stairs, raised in indignation: "Presentable?

Did she say *presentable*? I've cooked your dinner and washed it up, and now I'm washing Gregor's shirts, among other things. When people with nothing to busy them aren't presentable—"

"Are you referring to me?" came with an attempt at icy dignity from above.

"I am indeed."

Tramping footsteps back across the floor, and a door slammed. Karine continued heavily down the stairs. "Anything wrong, Karine?" whispered Lagerta through the crack in the door.

"They want rhubarb wine. There's none of their own left so they want some of ours. They had more bottles than we did, but—"

"We can put some more down soon, Karine. The rhubarb's lasting well."

"If we get round to it, we can," said Karine. "We're only human. And they might at least carry their ash out themselves, the little they have to do. Look at it."

With disgust Karine displayed a sizeable ashtray, filled to the brim and topped with cigarette ends.

"Weeping and gnashing of teeth, and that Kaia from the chemist's to bring consolation. We know what sort of consolation she has to give. You go back again, Miss Lagerta, don't you bother. Gregor has to come home, it's one of those days. I expect she's back on the couch again already, she was lying there when I went up, not fit to get anything for herself. But she could run after me as far as the door and give cheek, all right."

"Please Karine, take up the wine."

"That's what I'm going to do, take up the wine. For your sake and for Gregor's, I've no estimation for anyone else in this house. They shall have their wine."

"She isn't well today." Lagerta tried to adopt her permanent role of conciliator.

"Not well? I wish all of us were so well. But people who chain-smoke and stay up all night and are never out except when they're shut up in a car and don't know what to be at and stuff themselves with poison may well be a bit under the weather now and again. Presentable! She said 'presentable'! Some folks ought to be careful what words they use. *She* looks like—I can't describe what she looks like. You go and lie down, Miss Lagerta, or go for a walk in the sunshine. That Kaia will have to go home for supper if for nothing else, for decency's sake, and then it'll be quiet as we know. But those youngsters may be back any time now, they only went to the north side to look for an accordion, I heard them talking about it."

Karine turned in the kitchen doorway: "I peeped into their bedroom as I went by—the door was open. You should see what it's like in *there*. Beds not made for days, clothes and shoes all over the place, one big mess. As usual. That was when the young madam came for me. She didn't like me looking in."

"Now then, Karine."

But Karine turned once more. "Our Jonas came like an answer to prayer, didn't he? Who knows, perhaps he was. There's much that is hidden from us."

And she went. She did not see the tired, affectionate little smile on Lagerta's face.

IV

"Is there anyone with you?" asked Jonas from the door, looking round him in some astonishment.

"No." Lagerta turned away from the western window where she had been standing, her thoughts elsewhere, watching the movement of the sun towards the north, where the peaks were lower and the expanse of sky wider. "Who would be here at this time of day? We can't expect Gregor for a long time yet."

"I was positive you were talking to someone. You said something just as I came in."

"There's nobody here, as you see." The colour mounted in Lagerta's cheeks and receded as quickly as it had come. "A voice from the road perhaps. People are out late in this fine weather and the veranda door is open. Sounds carry so strangely."

"I could have sworn it was you. But there you are, it couldn't have been. Well, here I am again, and now I'll stay until Gregor comes. I found out that he's being ferried over, he's chugging along in Rasmus's old motorboat now. They're hardly likely to arrive before early morning. Good of Rasmus to take him as late as this. Does it inconvenience you to have me here? You can go to bed, in fact you should."

"I'm too restless to go to bed, Jonas. Have you had any supper? Or will you have something to drink?"

"I have had supper, thank you, and I don't want anything for the time being. It's quiet upstairs, I notice."

"What do you expect when Kaia has been here? Even the children disappear, goodness knows where."

"Poor kids," said Jonas involuntarily.

"Yes indeed, Jonas, poor kids."

"Thoroughly wayward."

"But don't tell me it's Gregor's fault. If it's anybody's fault it's mine. I assure you I've thought it all out. Gregor was so uncertain of his feelings at that time that he asked for my advice. It takes a lot to do that, young people don't like asking their relatives about such things. And after all, I should seem like a close relative to both of you. I was so glad he could even contemplate a new relationship. You know, I had watched him—"

61

"You couldn't have known what Dondi was like. I was quite taken with her myself to begin with."

"As a woman I should have known better, something should have told me. 'Do you like her, Lagerta?' he asked me one day. It's the only thing he has ever asked me about really in his whole life, and the fact that he did should have warned me. What a fool I am!"

"Now you're talking sense. So you're a fool are you?"

"Oh yes, Jonas, I am a fool," admitted Lagerta. But she pulled herself together and said with an effort, as if picking up something unpleasant: "Who was that this afternoon?"

"Someone Andersen is going to marry. An honest person as far as I know. Rough and impetuous, with a reputation for it in fact, but hard-working and clever and certainly too good for someone like Mr. Andersen. Well—that's her own look-out. I should have realized she might interfere. What a good thing—"

"—distances are short, isn't it? Thank you for coming, Jonas."

"So you know Karine—?"

"I saw her through the window. Is it *true* what that woman was saying?"

"It is and it isn't. It's pushed to extremes of course, as anything of that sort is. They probably think they've got us under their thumbs now, she and Andersen, and that we're so afraid of gossip that we'll agree to anything. But the gossip—"

"It probably started a long time ago," said Lagerta with resignation.

"Frankly, I should think you're the only one still in the dark. And Gregor, perhaps, he's preoccupied enough. Great-grandmamma smells a rat, if I judge her correctly. I had hoped to spare you as long as I could, I hadn't taken Mrs. Styrsvold's enterprise into consideration."

"Why should I be spared? I've had a feeling for quite a time that something was wrong. As if we had something dangerous in the house, something quite erratic."

"That's precisely what we do have. Something so foreign to us that we'll never be able to make it out."

"Well then, Jonas—what if we tried some kind of modern treatment? A good psychiatrist, for instance?"

"There you go again, that's all that's lacking. Off to Southern Norway year after year for this so-called analysis. I say so-called, though I must admit my ignorance in such matters. It seems to me that if anyone is to be analysed a certain amount of self-blame has to enter into it, and if so Dondi would give up that particular medicine-man, you can bet your life on it. Then she'd rush off to another who would get just as far. If you really want to throw that money of yours down the drain, get her started on something like that. We'd have some peace here as long as it lasted, but at a price, far too high a price in the long run. Besides, she's scared of it herself, or she'd have seen to it a long time ago."

But Lagerta was following her own train of thought: "She is so peculiar sometimes."

"Play-acting," said Jonas. "She puts it on to frighten us. Shall I tell you what Dondi's illness is? Egoism, childish demands on life, and the sulks because life doesn't answer to her expectations. The only cure for such a condition is life itself. If it were to clip her wings just once, then, who knows—? That's what Dr. Berven thinks too, though he doesn't exactly say so."

Jonas was standing at one of the windows that looked out over the fjord. He always preferred to stand at windows or to pace the floor, as if staying indoors made him restless. Smoke from picnic fires rose from several places along the shingle left uncovered by the tide, and from the mountains on the other side of the water. Boats chugged along the shore, and behind them golden stripes barred the green, sun-warmed reflections in the sea. Many people were out of doors in the mild, still evening.

"Damnable that it should all blow up in this weather, when we get so little summer up here. We could have been out in the boat, Lagerta, as we used to in the old days."

But Lagerta was still wrapped up in her own thoughts: "Berven's old, remember."

"And experienced, and he understands his patients. He's a little too kind to prescribe exactly what Dondi has just set her mind on having. But he knows he's only being asked as a matter of form. She gets whatever she's talked you into. And then he probably thinks of Gregor whom he helped into the world, and of what will spare him most. I know he's advised Dondi to get a divorce."

"Has he?" said Lagerta forlornly.

"She made a worse outcry than ever. She probably will this time too, but we shall have to put up with it. Speaking about analysis, that reminds me—Kaia from the chemist's has got hold of that foreigner. Do you know who I mean?"

"I've heard him mentioned. What sort of a man is he?"

"A refugee from one of the Baltic states, and as such presumably deserving of sympathy. Though there are all sorts among them too. I don't like the look of him myself; cool customer if I'm not mistaken. Makes himself out to be a psychiatrist and analyst, calls himself Dr. But nowadays there are swarms of people who presume to meddle with the mechanisms of their fellow human beings without being medically qualified; with their impulses and emotions especially. No-one will convince me that they're not satisfying their own emotions to some extent, and their inquisitiveness as well. You see how

64

reactionary I am. I have the greatest suspicion of all that sort of thing."

"Perhaps too much, Jonas. We're out of things up here."

"Now you're in the danger zone again. Kaia might be sitting up there finding Dondi an easy convert, and Dondi might phone down to you . . . I must tell you at once, the fellow isn't allowed to practise here."

"Oh well, in that case . . . Anyway, Kaia left some time ago."

Jonas turned from the window, busied himself with his pipe, filled it and lighted it. "For my part," he said between puffs, "I believe in the well-aimed, old-fashioned box on the ears. It does far more good than all that tinkering. Not if people are really ill, of course, but if they're perverse and unreasonable. It should have the same effect as knocking yourself hard on the edge of a table; gives you something to think about and you keep a good look out the next time."

"It's not as simple as all that. I don't believe in it."

"I know you don't."

"And you consider *yourself* capable of deciding who's ill and who isn't?"

"In this case, most certainly."

Pause.

"Would you have preferred it if I hadn't come?" asked Jonas after a while.

"I'm glad you came," said Lagerta warmly.

"You know how much I enjoy coming."

"Coming!" Lagerta was suddenly angry. "You shouldn't just come, you should live here. If you knew how it distresses me that you should be living down there in the shade. Up here we get all the sun there is, morning, afternoon, evening and night."

She looked around her at the large room, where the

light from a slanting ray of sunshine now reached high up the walls and into the corners of the ceiling. It possessed an eerie quality, very different from the daytime.

"At this time of year there's always sun in the room from one direction or another," she continued. "There's almost too much."

"Oh no. And we have sun in town as well, you know."

"The shadows fall early down there. And it's so empty in the evenings, especially in weather like this. Everybody out somewhere. If someone walks down the street you can hear him all over town."

"I'm all right down there."

"You prefer it to living here. I understand that."

"Well, life is made up of alternatives," said Jonas, "and that's especially true since the war. I like it in my two small rooms. I console myself now and then with the thought that they all stood there at their high desks: Great-grandfather, Grandfather, and Father. I seem to remember Father standing at his when I was very small. We got different paraphernalia later on of course. But at that time the office was in there and the shop was—"

"Console yourself for what?" interrupted Lagerta, looking up.

"Oh, I don't know. For life's misfortunes."

"Perhaps you should have replaced Øyen after all?" suggested Lagerta cautiously. "Taken on another man?"

"Another? What are you thinking of? I shall have to go on being my own Øyen. A girl in the office and a man on the quay are all the firm can manage at the moment. We have almost nothing left besides the freighting business. We don't want anything more either. But to get you to understand that I'd have to give you a course of instruction. We're on our beam ends."

"We can't be the only ones at a time like this, surely?"

"No. But there are degrees, you know."

"No, I don't know. I don't know anything about it. But I can't help wondering sometimes why you don't—sell up and—go away, and . . . "

"Sell up!" said Jonas amused. "You don't do things by halves, do you?"

"I admit I don't know what I'm talking about. But as time passes, I feel more and more strongly that you ought really to have been doing something quite different in a completely different place. Especially since it became almost only the freighting. The shop must have been more interesting."

"It appealed to the imagination more than those two small offices, it's true."

"I remember how funny I thought the sign was on the outside wall, Jonas."

" 'Trader in coal and ship's biscuits, cod-liver oil and dried fish.' Surprisingly enough, it's still there."

"Yes, but almost illegible," said Lagerta, livening up. "And do you remember all the Lapp clothes lying so bright on the shelves, red and yellow and green and blue. And the balls of wood, for wool, that came from Russia, with that delicate, dull gilding which glistened in the dark; and the tiny, thick window panes; and everything hanging from the ceiling making it even darker, sea boots and sou'westers and dippers . . . And it smelt so good, an absolutely unique, complex, well-stored fragrance, which I discovered consisted of spices and ropes and tar and leather. I had never been in a shop like it. And then Øyen, glimpsed through the office door, quaint and old-fashioned as well, with his pen behind his ear. But then you suddenly began to wind it all up."

"Yes, Father had gone, times had changed," said Jonas.

He stood looking at her pensively "Even Øyen considered it wisest to sell up."

"Times are always changing," said Lagerta sadly, as if to herself, and Jonas hastened to guide the conversation back to the pleasant turn it had taken. "You don't remember the Russian sea-captains, I suppose?"

"No, but Great-grandmamma has described them so often that I can picture them very clearly, in their blue quilted jackets and pudding-basin haircuts, with their wives always two paces in the rear, wearing old-fashioned, flowered frocks with skirt panels. And they came up to supper occasionally, bringing sweets and candied fruit and souchong, and your father and grandfather spoke Russian to them. Great-grandmamma was given some beautiful Chinese cups too. What a pity all that came to an end, Jonas."

"It's a pity a great many things come to an end," said Jonas. "But as a matter of fact you didn't like the cod-liver oil or the fish smells. You went about holding a handkerchief to your nose, and groaning."

"The fish smell was only on the wharf, and as for the cod-liver oil, we never noticed that except when there was an east wind. Now there's a smell of herring oil with almost every sort of wind. And what about the timber, *that* smelt really good. Great-grandmamma says that in the Russian traders' time the ships from Archangel were loaded to the gunwales with planks and deal, and if the wind was in the right direction the scent would reach you on shore before you could see the boat through your binoculars."

"Great-grandmamma's imagination was carrying her away a little at that point, she had a weakness for the subject. But I didn't think you had paid much attention to it."

"Oh, of course. Only I had so much else to think about."

"How about making us a good cup of coffee, Lagerta, and then I'll tell you about Great-great-grandfather's time, when we had our own merchant ships plying from our own wharves. Not only to Hamburg and Bremen and places like that, but to Naples and Venice and even, my dear, to Rio. That's where we went for coffee, as a matter of fact.

"*American* coffee," he added, when Lagerta hesitated. "Good and strong. I expect we shall need it."

"We had coffee after lunch, Jonas. We must have some left for Gregor when he comes. Good coffee in case Rasmus comes with him."

"Rasmus won't do that so early in the morning. He'll sleep in the labourers' quarters at his brother's place. It's not like you to be so economical."

"I am with coffee. We haven't much left."

"And you'd rather keep what we have for Gregor. After all, writers must have coffee. I expect he asks you for it."

"Occasionally," admitted Lagerta.

"I swear I'll get you some more. From America. Soon."

"You're not a conjurer. The coffee will arrive when it's due, no sooner and no later. They can't send as much as they'd like."

"I'm not a conjurer?" said Jonas, now positively hilarious. "I may say so myself, but I've conjured up quite a few things in my time. There are limits to my powers, but coffee—I can conjure up coffee, you may depend on it."

He stood with his hands in his trouser pockets, swaying from the knees to emphasize his assertions. He looked almost intoxicated.

"Nincompoop." Lagerta smiled a wry, indulgent smile, the kind with which women greet bold and frivolous masculine whims, while nevertheless giving in to them. And she went.

Jonas obviously intended to keep the conversation to safe topics. He conversed with Lagerta so eagerly and incessantly about old ships and their exploits, shipping concerns and pioneers of local history, that finally she remarked, quite exhausted: "I often wonder whether you should take more part in the life of the community, as your family did. Even your father was an alderman, and he was at the head of all sorts of organizations. He was a consul as well. Wouldn't something like that interest you?"

"No," said Jonas. "It wouldn't interest me."

"But why not?"

"That's more than I can tell you."

Lagerta surveyed him thoughtfully for a moment. Medium height, much smaller than Gregor, thick-set and strong, his tan makes his grey eyes look lighter than they really are. He sits at a desk, an office desk. Ought he to be sitting there really?

Jonas was looking thoughtful too. He said: "A real businessman would have got more out of it than I do, even in times like these. But it won't come to a complete standstill."

"I don't mean to suggest you're not good at it, only that perhaps you may sometimes hanker after something else now and again."

"I hanker after fresh air and exercise," said Jonas curtly. "And I get it, in my humble fashion. I walk in the mountains every Sunday, summer and winter. Unless it's snowing, or drizzling, or pouring with rain. And as

70

for rain—I've nothing against rain when all's said and done. And then I row a little in the evenings; soon I shall be the only person in town doing it. They all have motor boats now."

"I see you sometimes through the binoculars."

"So you still use them?"

"Now and again, just out of habit. It's easy to recognize the boat; it's the only one of the old-fashioned type left."

"Do you never feel like coming with me?" asked Jonas, turning towards her. "Do you remember how, long ago, when you had put Gregor to bed, we sometimes stayed up all night, just drifting in the boat until early morning?

"It's a long time since we stayed up together in the midnight sun, you and I," he continued, preventing her from speaking. "Do you remember all the fish we caught? Do you remember the time we got more than seventy coalfish and codling? They wouldn't stop biting, the fjord boiled with fish leaping in the sun. You were in despair. 'The cat won't be able to eat one tenth of it,' you said, and: 'I expect Karine will give notice.' But we had a memorable fish soup for dinner and Karine is still with us."

"Yes, thank heaven. How would we manage without her?"

"You may well ask."

"But we're getting old, Jonas, Karine and the rest of us. Myself especially . . . "

"Are you afraid that two old people in an ancient relic of a boat will be a laughing stock?"

"You know I'm not."

"You've been going out far too little during the past few years. You hardly ever go down to town. Great-grandmamma insists that you're fretting so much about everything up here that you *daren't* go out. Things aren't as bad as that, surely?"

"No, of course not, Jonas."

"I'm not so sure," said Jonas speculatively. And a quiet little remark slipped out: "What about your passion for Gregor?"

"My passion?" repeated Lagerta in amazement.

"Not in any undesirable sense you understand," said Jonas, embarrassed at his somewhat unfortunate choice of word. "I hope we're still allowed to consider maternal passion normal and respectable?"

"Maternal passion? I don't like the word passion at all. There's something hysterical and extravagant about it. And my feelings for Gregor aren't extravagant or hysterical. Do you really know what you're talking about?" she concluded rather tartly. "After all, you are a man."

"Forgive me if I used an objectionable word. Of course I realize that Gregor, who was so small when—"

"Yes, he was small," said Lagerta angrily. "And ever since he grew up life has passed over him like a storm, it's devastated him. We've got to remember that, we've got to make allowances for it."

"We have remembered it and we've made allowances for it as much as we possibly could, and more," said Jonas. He too was impatient now. "I've often had my doubts as to whether we went the right way about it. Today—or rather tonight—"

"What if I were to help them once more, Jonas. One last time—in my own way. And in the way Gregor wants. You've said sometimes: 'Supposing he really has something ready and waiting, something really good'."

"That's exactly when he must be rescued, Lagerta, if anything is to come of it. And who knows what Gregor wants? Do you think he knows himself?"

"Yes, I do," said Lagerta. And she muttered something about selling 'those infernal securities'.

"Their value isn't high at the moment. They wouldn't realize much, if they realized anything at all."

"Then they can't be worth holding on to either."

"Lagerta! They are all you have. And they may go up again. Have you never heard of shares going up and down?"

"Yes, of course. But when we get to that part of it I get confused."

Jonas made no reply. He said drily: "Briefly, you're in no position to make a noose for your own neck just now. And a good thing too," he added emphatically. "Couldn't be better."

"Good? When the only happiness I get out of life is helping Gregor? My only 'passion', as you put it."

"I wish I could fathom why it is the only one," said Jonas, half to himself. He had turned away from her, but Lagerta heard him perfectly and, in spite of her usual calm, lost her temper.

"Of course you can't fathom it. Because you have none yourself, all you have is the firm!" She stopped short. "I'm sorry, Jonas, I am unreasonable. What do I know of you and your life? But things could have been different for you. *You* could have been the successful one of the family. Had a family yourself. A charming wife, delightful children—How I've wished for that, Jonas."

"Why should you suddenly bring *that* up?" said Jonas.

"You may well ask. I detest interfering in other people's affairs, I detest other people interfering in mine. But today is the kind of day when everything seems miserable and hopeless and—"

"Thank God you always understood what human freedom was, and respected it," said Jonas. "I've loved you for that all these years."

"I didn't mean to intrude now, either."

"No, but to serve you right, here's a disagreeable question in return. You said you wished I had had a family. Beyond that, did you ever think about me at all?"

"But my dear Jonas!"

"Of course I don't mean to imply that you neglected me. Clothes and—socks always mended—and understanding when I wanted something, you were wonderful. All I mean is that Gregor always played the biggest part and—and put the rest of us a bit in the shade."

"He needed me most."

"Yes, and if it hadn't been for him I suppose you'd never have come here? I can understand your coming, Lagerta, all things considered. But that you should have stayed—on and on although we grew up so many, many years ago! I suppose you're still anxious about Gregor, and you'll never stop being anxious about him. And you thought about me too? Now and again you noticed that I existed."

"Now you're being unkind, Jonas. And unreasonable. It wasn't like that at all."

"I don't expect it seemed so to you."

"It shouldn't have seemed so to you either. Were you really jealous of your little brother?"

"Who wasn't I jealous of?" said Jonas unintentionally. Lagerta looked at him in astonishment. "To think that I never noticed anything," she said wonderingly. And Jonas replied with a trace of bitterness: "No, you never 'noticed' anything."

He changed the subject abruptly: "Don't you find the landscape—cold—up here? Cold and bare?"

Lagerta, still a little astonished, replied vaguely: "Not on a summer day like this. Then it's—radiant—don't you think? And it's magnificent all the year round, even in bad weather."

"Yes, it is, magnificent and cold. And most true to itself in bad weather, with draperies of mist hanging up here and there as protection against the long distances. That's the kind of weather we have mostly. How many 'summer days' do we get? Fourteen on the average. No —trees are the thing, tall trees."

"Trees in France," said Lagerta, waking up.

"All right, in France. Avenues, spreading treetops, green arches, the humming of bees, sunshine through a roof of leaves, fragrance, warmth—evening air like the sum of all the perfumes of France."

"You're getting quite lyrical, Jonas. Not like you at all."

"All of us are unlike ourselves at times, I suppose, and talk about things there's no point in discussing. But what about you, Lagerta? You once thought of moving south for good, of taking up your painting again, of living your own life at last."

"I live my own life," said Lagerta. "Are you determined to get rid of me, you and Great-grandmamma? She asked me the same thing this morning in this very room. She does it every few years."

"You know we don't want to get rid of you."

"When Gregor got married the first time I thought about it. Now I'm not needed any longer, I thought. But then so much happened. He was widowed almost at once. Then he married again."

"And lived in Oslo for several years."

"I couldn't make up my mind to go, Jonas. To tell you the truth, I was anxious all the time. A writer you know—They had to have somewhere to go, supposing . . . "

Jonas was silent. Then he said: "It must often be lonely and dull for you. Whom have we associated with in recent years? No-one. Kaia from the chemist's. Our old friends moved south a long time ago, we don't make new ones because of Dondi and Dondi's children. Understandably enough. They're notorious all over town."

"We have nothing to do with Kaia."

"She runs in and out. That's more than anyone else does."

"It's best not to have any acquaintances," said Lagerta. "As far as I'm concerned," she added, "and as things are at present. But I'm sorry for Dondi."

"Dondi! Good God, what didn't you do for her to begin with? Dragged one young couple here after another, gave parties. And what came of it? Scenes and quarrels and tears. Finally Kaia turned up. She suited Dondi, however that friendship may have come about. Across the counter at the chemist's probably, though Kaia ought not to be mixed up in it. But who knows what she's mixed up in? No, Lagerta, we haven't isolated Dondi, Dondi has isolated us. Even Gregor went surprisingly far for the sake of Dondi's social life, and all he normally wants is peace and quiet. Nothing came of it but rows."

"You said 'lonely and dull', Jonas. It's lonely and dull for you. Why don't you go abroad this autumn? Before the winter comes? That trip before the war did you such a lot of good."

"I can't afford to travel."

"Oh surely? You're not ruined. It's not a bad idea to invest your money in a little extravagance now and then. You need to get away."

"I'm turning into an old fogey, you mean? That's the fate of a good many people as far north as this."

"It won't happen to you."

"It has happened to me," said Jonas submissively. "Hadn't you noticed? And of course I'm stingy as you know."

"Stingy?" said Lagerta guiltily. "No, Jonas. But you are careful. 'Sensible'," she added in inverted commas in order to improve on her remark.

"I am stingy. You've thought so plenty of times. Thought so and forked out yourself. I let you fork out for my own brother, I was so stingy."

"You know perfectly well that I've never thought of it in that way."

"Still, if we're to come out of this affair decently, we may perhaps be able to thank my stinginess for it. If matters are to be cleared up—and they must and shall be —it will cost money. A lot of money for people like us."

"If we come out of it," said Lagerta. "If we ever come out of it, I almost said."

"Well—the children will grow up. Then, by God, they'll have to look after themselves."

"Dondi never will, you mean?"

"I don't see how anyone like Dondi could grow up."

"But what shall we have achieved then, Jonas?"

"A few years' peace for Gregor. A little tranquillity for Gregor. An opportunity for him to collect himself. That's all we two can do for him.

"If it's any use our helping him any more," added Jonas under his breath. "I hope so," he said, a little louder. "Then you could think about getting away too, Lagerta," he added yet again, tentatively.

"Oh, never mind about me."

"It's late in the day, I admit, but not *too* late. Not for someone like you."

"Someone like me," said Lagerta bitterly, dropping her voice. "Someone like me! You've obviously been talking to Great-grandmamma today. It's one of her obsessions."

"Never mind. I know something of what sort of a person you are too. The older I get, the better I know.

77

Imagine leaving your youth and your art behind you, and burying yourself up here."

"It was no burial," said Lagerta tartly.

"It must have been. Especially at that time. When I got away from here I began to realize how you must have felt. Even if you get no further than Southern Norway you come to see how cold and harsh nature is up here, how dependent on the light. It looks like theatrical scenery on which someone has tried to economize. With the sun's spotlight, or the moon's, directly on it, it can look quite attractive, but otherwise . . . And then the endless distances, the narrow conditions."

"I do wish you and Great-grandmamma would stop thinking I've buried myself here. On the contrary," said Lagerta nervously, with some impatience. "You can't imagine what that little boy meant to me—no-one could imagine it. I became very fond of both of you, but Gregor was so tiny, only a few months old."

"Yes, I suppose he was the child you had wanted? Even an elderly male can understand that."

Lagerta picked up her sewing, but let it fall into her lap again at once. "Gregor is my own child," she said quickly and calmly, as if powerless to stop herself. "Not that I brought him into the world, of course."

"No—unless you and Mother practised sorcery."

"The sorcery came about of itself, Jonas. As sorcery does," said Lagerta. She picked up her sewing again, made a couple of stitches in it without paying much attention, then stuck in the needle securely as if to ensure it against further molestation.

"Sorcery," said Jonas. "Why should they want to go out in a heavy ten-oared boat, on a dark night, in that weather? The barometer pointed to storm."

"Your mother wanted to get back to the baby," said Lagerta. "They must have thought they'd reach home before the storm broke. They had experienced sailors on board."

"They should have been experienced enough to know better. But if we're to interpret a capsizing as sorcery . . ."

"That's how I interpret it."

"All right. But you were so young, barely twenty-two. To put it bluntly, think of all the children you could have had yourself."

"Could I?"

"Why ever not?"

"Well, I didn't have them, that's all," said Lagerta, so severely discouraging this time that Jonas looked worried for a moment.

"Forgive me," he said. "I don't want to be inquisitive. But I can't stop wondering about so many things that happened at that time. The relationship between Father and Mother for instance. I remember them well, I can remember the atmosphere being tense sometimes without being able to make out why. Children are quick to notice things like that, but still—I was very fond of them both, I believe. At any rate I was unhappy if something didn't seem quite right. There was never a cross word, and yet —And then they went and had another child when I was already thirteen. Was it accidental or did it mean something? I have some recollection that everything was sweetness and light just before Gregor was born. And afterwards as well—until the disaster."

"Don't let's go into that, Jonas."

"No, we won't. And I don't suppose you know much more about them than I do. But I hope I may be allowed to say how good it was of you to come."

"You said that very nicely on my fiftieth birthday."

"And I'm not to be allowed to repeat it occasionally? The older I get, the more heroic I think you've been."

"I, heroic!" said Lagerta, her voice icy with scorn.

79

"Yes. Heroic. Good Lord, surely you can admit it to yourself just a little. Your modesty—in anyone else I'd think it was false."

"It is false too, you'll see," said Lagerta, suddenly on the verge of tears.

"Stuff and nonsense. Come, come, Lagerta, I really didn't mean to hurt you."

"I know. I'm just tired," said Lagerta, drying her tears. "Don't take any notice of me, Jonas."

"I expect I shall go on crying," she said, cried a little more and dried her tears yet again.

"To begin with. Then it'll be all right, you'll see . . . Do you know what I remember most clearly about the early days when you were here? Your speaking in a high, clear voice like that. It must have been dismal here after what had happened. It was as if you were trying to get us to think about something else all the time."

"I expect I had that kind of voice. After all, I was— young."

"I don't think so. Your voice is naturally deep."

"Do you really remember my coming, Jonas?"

"Do you need to ask? I was almost fourteen. You cried at first of course. Then you began to talk in that high voice. And you were so nice. Even then you were *much* too nice."

"It wasn't difficult. You were nice too. Such a very nice little boy."

"I?—an egoist trying to get into your good graces."

"The things you say!"

"That's how it was, Lagerta, that's how it was."

"I remember," said Lagerta, who had recovered, "how much I wanted you to call me Auntie. After all, it would have been natural at your age, and I should have felt a little more dignified. But no. 'Mother' wouldn't have been right, neither of us approved of that."

"No, heaven help us! And as for 'Auntie'—"

"Your mother's sister *is* your aunt. But I had to put up with being called Lagerta by you as well as by everybody else, even by Gregor when he grew up."

"I couldn't bring myself to say anything else," said Jonas curtly.

"'Was it—difficult for you to get used to me, Jonas? I'd rather not say 'put up with me', but—"

"No, of course not," said Jonas.

"—since you didn't want to call me 'Auntie'? We can surely talk about it openly now we're both of us old?"

"Ugh!" said Jonas. " 'Auntie' and 'Mother'! You were Lagerta."

"Just then you sounded exactly as you used to when you were a boy, Jonas," laughed Lagerta.

"Did I? Well, it was always just as hateful every time you mentioned the subject. I don't understand this ambition to be an aunt. As if it wasn't good enough to be Lagerta? Better, it seems to me. Surely you realize what it means to us all? But no, every now and again you bring up this aunt business again."

"I was inexperienced, you know, and unused to—to children . . . Perhaps I wanted to give myself a little authority. That was foolish of course. But did you really feel neglected, Jonas? Gregor was still a baby, after all. You were already grown up."

"Lord, yes, ready to be confirmed and go into long trousers. I don't know that I wanted too much maternal solicitude."

"That's just what I thought I understood. And we became such good friends. When there was any difficulty over Gregor I often discussed it with you as with a friend."

"Maybe, but without listening to me. You spoiled Gregor terribly."

"Perhaps I did. I had a soft spot for him. But so did you. You loved your little brother. How extraordinary that we should be talking about this now."

"There are a lot of things we two haven't talked about," said Jonas under his breath.

"Yes, that's true, isn't it Jonas?" said Lagerta, livening up. "I wanted nothing so much as your confidence, but I was afraid of forcing myself on you. Was I wrong in that? Nowadays they say you get 'complexes' from what doesn't come out."

"If we're to believe the new gospel, yes. In that case God knows what complexes you've got. The fact is we hold our tongues a great deal in this house, and it's a long time since I heard you laugh, for instance, a good, hearty laugh. I don't think much of that short, little laugh you come out with from time to time. Don't you remember how we used to laugh together in the old days, when life got back to normal again after all the mourning and sadness? I used to come home from school and tell you hair-raising stories of the pranks we boys had been up to. Once I came home with the worst bad conduct mark. You tried to look severe, but you couldn't manage it. In the end we laughed so much we were bent double. It was the time I stood behind Hoem holding the hat over his head while he was filling out the register, and it dropped right down over his ears. It wasn't his hat, it was Blekerud's, and it was much too big."

"Great-grandmamma laughed too."

"She was a good sort. But she's so old now, poor little thing. And how about your dancing, Lagerta? Nobody could dance as well as you when you could be persuaded on to the floor. You did exhibition dancing too, with Captain Buvik. The two of you danced the tango beautifully. It was for the Red Cross."

"Oh, my dancing," said Lagerta uneasily. "It wasn't

good for me to dance," she said compulsively, dropping her voice.

"Why ever not?"

"It made me—restless . . . I—it wasn't suitable."

"No, I suppose not. It became less lively here after a time too. It beats me how you held out. It isn't as if you had had no choice."

"I had my livelihood here."

"Livelihood?"

"Yes, food and a roof over my head and—"

"And you call that your livelihood?"

"It became so natural after a while. I didn't think about it any more. My home was here, Jonas. And that was my livelihood."

"How like you, where practical issues are concerned. You simply don't see them. You must be one of those people who are determined to sacrifice themselves, come what may. Your youth, your painting, you sacrificed everything."

"Stop this talk about sacrifice," said Lagerta sharply. "You brought it up earlier today too. Great-grandmamma is always bringing it up. I sacrificed nothing. As for my painting, I don't suppose you've ever seen those life studies propped up against the wall in the attic?"

"Yes I have. They're at least as good as other work that's being done, and better than a lot of it. And you were young, you had scarcely started."

" 'Started', yes. That's all there was to it. I wasn't the right type. You need more than a bit of talent. You talk about sacrifice. Art demands sacrifices, from a woman at any rate, greater ones than I was capable of making. The men—I was never capable of making sacrifices, whether here or in Paris, only of saving my bacon. Don't torment me, Jonas. You torment me when you say such things. Everything's wretched today, it's one of those days when

I feel nothing but disgust for myself—when I feel cowardly, spiteful, venomous. And here are you talking about sacrifice."

Lagerta had spoken choking back her anger. She regained control and said: "It *was* distressing to have to leave Paris, more distressing than anyone could imagine. I thought I would die. But Great-grandmamma couldn't have been left alone up here with that little child, and with Great-grandfather helpless after his stroke, and it was good for me. Very good for me. And everything happened at once, that meaningless shipwreck and his illness. Perhaps the one was connected with the other—who knows?"

She hid her face in her hands for a moment, as if trying not to see something. Then she said: "Coming up here was a violent experience, Jonas, I don't know what to compare it with—being killed and slowly coming alive again. I was not myself for a while . . . "

"Hm," said Jonas.

"I know I made a decision—the sort you make when you have to throw yourself out of the window so as to save yourself."

"To save yourself?" repeated Jonas. "From what?"

Lagerta was silent for a little. Then she said thoughtfully: "From becoming a slave, I suppose."

"A slave! To whom? To what?"

"To myself. Plenty of people are."

"Now you're talking in riddles."

"Am I?"

"It seems so to me. You a slave? To your craving for self-sacrifice, perhaps, to your duty. But you won't admit that, so we'd better not talk about it."

But Lagerta seemed to be talking to herself: "I came to myself one day with the little child on my lap and—began to live again. I felt almost rehabilitated."

84

"Rehabilitated? That's another of your words. You have such fixed ideas, Lagerta. You're far too tenderhearted, far too conscientious."

"Are you taunting me, Jonas?"

"Taunting you?"

"You don't mean it, I know. Now don't let's talk about it any more."

At this point Lagerta burst openly into tears, sobbed loudly a couple of times, pulled herself together, became calm again, and dried her cheeks. "I must be a little unbalanced tonight," she said.

"In the first place you're dead tired. You should have gone to bed, and left this showdown with Gregor to me. All this hullabaloo with Dondi—one of these days it'll be too much for you."

Lagerta was not listening to him; she sat lost in thought. Suddenly she said: "Did you ever hear of Landru? Do you remember him?"

"Landru—Landru? Yes. Yes, of course. A murderer of the first order, he murdered women. I heard about him many years ago."

"Many years ago, towards the end of the first world war. A good while before I went to Paris. But I came to know people who had followed the case closely; it attracted a lot of attention, in spite of the circumstances. I often came to think of Landru later on in life."

"That mass murderer?"

"The mass murderer. He was so correct, Jonas. Even during the trial none of them was as correct as he. Not a word, not an intonation, not a gesture, that were not those of a gentleman."

"Well and good, but what has this to do with you?"

"Outward propriety may have very little to do with the inner man. It may be entirely misleading."

"And this is so in your case?"

"Yes. It's a shield that I have. I need it. And I know I shan't lose it here."

Lagerta now spoke quite calmly. "I'm the kind of person who finds it easy to act recklessly," she said.

"You—?"

"Yes, I walk into traps, life's traps. My only defence is to side-step them."

"And here you felt safe?"

"Yes," said Lagerta, a little vacantly, a little absently. "Here I felt safe."

Jonas was silent. He paced up and down, stood at the window, looked at the clock. He found nothing to say for the time being, and sought refuge in mere commonplaces: "We shan't see the boat for a long while yet."

But Lagerta continued as if talking to herself: "Some days you notice unexpected things. Or they're suddenly revealed to you. Your life is illuminated far back from a new angle. Just as if, towards evening, after a storm, a rift may appear in the clouds . . . Everything looks strange and frightening, but you know it's the truth."

"A false light," said Jonas. "A poisonous light, completely misleading."

"No. A true light. A terrible light. But I mustn't get hysterical on top of everything else."

Lagerta made a helpless gesture with her hand across her face.

"You won't get hysterical."

"Oh yes, I shall. And wicked."

"Your wickedness—" said Jonas, laughing.

"Don't minimize it, Jonas. You have no idea how wicked I am. Poisoned with malice."

Suddenly her face became distorted. She almost whispered: "Have you noticed what an echo of Dondi Gregor has become?"

"Have I noticed? I was surprised you hadn't noticed it too. But you evidently had."

"Noticed it—noticed it—? I didn't want to, I couldn't bear to admit it. And Gregor's tone of voice—that grudging tone of his . . .

"As for that hole up there," she exclaimed bitterly, "it's nothing but a pig-sty. That Gregor, with his feeling for beauty, should have to live in it. But he probably doesn't notice it any more, and that's almost worse.

"He shouldn't be like this," she said angrily. "He was never like this before, he was a completely different person. So frank, so honest, so friendly, so wise. I pine for the days when he was twelve or thirteen years of age. The only thing he was reserved about was his writing. We could talk about so many things, and yet he was still a child. I—he was such a delight."

"And now he's shabby, frayed at the edges."

"You mustn't say shabby, Jonas. You've said it before today. It's such an ugly word. And it's not right."

But Jonas maintained that no other word would do. "Do you want examples?" he said.

"No," said Lagerta violently. And then, as if something snapped inside her, she almost shouted: "He is the child I betrayed, Jonas, the child I abandoned, gave away to others. Like any ordinary, simple girl, I let them take him out of my arms. They took him away."

She hid her face in her hands and wept aloud. Jonas attempted one of his awkward gestures which never came to anything. For a while he said nothing. Finally he managed to stammer out: "Lagerta—"

"Why am I talking about it," sobbed Lagerta. "I've never talked about it before . . . Up to now I've avoided becoming desperate. Is it to justify all my stupidities? Because they've caught up with me?

"They caught up with me a long time ago," she said

more calmly, drying her tears. "One does so many stupid things because of a guilty conscience—to make a good impression, I suppose . . . You wouldn't have believed such a thing of your refined, upright, admirable Lagerta, would you?" she said cuttingly.

"I don't believe it now either," said Jonas steadily.

"Do you think I'm making it up?"

"God knows what you're doing. You make everything sound worse than it is, at any rate. You're not yourself today. Which is only to be expected."

"I'm not out of my mind, Jonas. It's simply one of those days when I can see clearly. I abandoned my own child, and afterwards I tried to monopolize another in order to console myself—to make amends to myself. Nothing came of it. I am left empty-handed, as I deserve."

Jonas was at a loss. He said cautiously: "How can you expect me to believe *you* would abandon a child? You, who have always had such—integrity and—talent and—money of your own, and—It doesn't make sense, Lagerta."

"What doesn't make sense? Integrity you say? I was blinded with fear. I realized when it was too late that all I could do was accept the responsibility for it, and hold my tongue."

Tears overcame her again. "I hung around in cafés—I didn't know what to do with myself. I could have gone with anybody just to get away from myself for a while. I was out of my mind then, Jonas . . .

"Well—then came the disaster up here. Terrible as it was *I* profited by it. I had a little child in my arms again."

"Lagerta," repeated Jonas, utterly at a loss.

Lagerta dried her tears, silent tears that would not stop pouring down her cheeks. "You see, nearly thirty-two years ago things weren't the same as they are now. I'm not saying it as an excuse, there is no excuse. No mitigating circumstances even. I only mean—do you remember your grandparents on your mother's side?"

"Only vaguely," said Jonas.

"They were so—so irreproachable, so—so completely lacking in understanding of what life is really like. I suppose I made myself think it was out of pity for them that I did what I did, I hid behind thoughts like that. All that old nonsense. It was my life that was concerned, not theirs."

"And the child's father?" Jonas could not help asking.

"I didn't take him into account," said Lagerta curtly. "As for money—I didn't feel I owned my money. Others had dealt with it as far back as I could remember. I continued to let them deal with it and was grateful for what I got. They were prudent people, you see. Now and again they explained things to me which I couldn't grasp, about markets and stock exchange values and God knows what. I was bored to tears, I wouldn't stay and listen. I—"

"No, of course you wouldn't. Because then you'd have had to be practical like everyone else, and it wasn't in your nature."

"Perhaps so. I never thought about it. I was only aware of one thing at the time: that I would have to go home to two respectable people in a small town, prominent figures in the community, and say, 'Here I am back again with an illegitimate child.' They had allowed me to go away after much hesitation. It's a wonder they allowed me to go at all. I suppose they relied on my admirable upbringing which had included everything except for one single item. You have no idea how incredibly green a young girl could be in those days, Jonas. They warned one against so much, but never against oneself. Integrity, did you say I had integrity? I was merely cowardly, miserable, afraid. I could have got rid of the child in another way, I was given good advice. I couldn't bring myself to take it. But I could bring myself to give away a living child—"

"You would have come here to us in any case, Lagerta. You would have come when the accident happened. You're that kind of person."

"No, Jonas, no. I was as self-centred as I could possibly be. I had to go under completely before I had room in my head for a thought for others."

Pause.

"It was a little boy," she continued, staring in front of her with dry eyes, eyes that saw something a long way off. "I hid myself in another *quartier;* in Paris that's almost like emigrating to another part of the globe. I went to a midwife in the Rue d'Alésia. She 'disposed' of him for me."

Jonas turned paler and paler under his tan until he was almost yellow. He sat, clearly searching for something to say. But Lagerta was angry again. "Impractical," she said. "You talk of being impractical with money. People with guilty consciences like me do the most incredible things to redeem themselves in their own eyes and in the eyes of others, to be 'esteemed and 'respected'. It's just as well it does look like impracticality. Impracticality is a fine thing, self-forgetful and fine. You don't have to be ashamed of being impractical."

Jonas made no reply. "What a swine of a man to leave you to face it alone," he muttered finally.

"It was I who left of my own accord. And I've never regretted that, at any rate. Feelings can be operated away just like an appendix. One remark can be as effective as a knife. You feel empty afterwards, but that passes too. Even the scar disappears."

"I daren't think what you must have gone through," said Jonas hesitatingly.

"The first few years were the worst. I suppose I had what they call crises every now and then. I managed to keep them to myself, in spite of Great-grandmamma's clear-sightedness—She really is clear-sighted, Jonas."

"Yes, she is," said Jonas.

"But if at any time you thought I was unsociable—"

"I never thought so," said Jonas.

"I went to France once, I don't suppose you remember? Gregor was three, the little boy down there somewhat older. Some friends of mine had found out where he was, and they got permission for me to visit him on condition that I gave nothing away. He had been adopted, you see, by excellent people, and he was not to know that he wasn't their child. I made myself out to be from the city, staying in the Normandy countryside. I took toys and sweets with me. Something for him to wear as well, but I didn't give it him in the end. They looked as if they were comfortably off—they were well-to-do farmers—and I was afraid of offending them. So I brought it home again. Gregor had it instead. A little strawberry coloured sweater, if you remember. He looked so sweet in it. It was a really nice little sweater, bought at Bon Marché . . . "

"I don't remember that. But I do remember your going away and coming home again. I was afraid you were never coming back. What a journey it must have been for you."

"It was worse going, easier coming home. You see, he wasn't my little boy, he was somebody else's. A happy little boy, as far as I could tell, chubby and brown and confident. A lovely little boy, but so entirely somebody else's. He didn't need me. If I had found a pale little creature—"

Lagerta's voice failed her, but she mastered it again. "I didn't dare touch him. After all, I was a strange lady.

91

He didn't take much notice of me either. Just took his presents and was going to run off. He had to be told to say thank you. I barely had his hand in mine—at least I was able to feel him—I—On the way home I told myself over and over again that I ought to be truly thankful . . ."

Jonas did not see the shadow of something distant, something put behind her but never mastered, which was reflected for an instant in Lagerta's face. He sat looking up at the ceiling where the patch of midnight sun was moving further and further towards the corner of the house. Here it would shortly disappear behind the wall for a while, before reappearing through one of the many windows as ordinary morning sunshine. His eyes were hard and he looked worn with grief.

"I travelled home relieved and—and empty at the same time," continued Lagerta. "I felt as I imagine people feel when they have had a painful arm or leg amputated, they get used to living without it. They don't get rid of the pain, so I've heard, and I can well imagine it to be true. But I had nothing to worry about any more. And then when Gregor came running into my arms and seized me round the neck, beside himself with joy—after that, somehow it was only Gregor who meant anything to me. At the same time I came to understand more and more clearly what I had done. Oh Jonas, at times it was so distressing. It's distressing to this day."

Jonas still said nothing. Lagerta talked on in the automatic voice that follows tears. "For a long time I had felt I was looking after the little boy in France when I looked after Gregor. After that journey he really was Gregor. On the way home the thought struck me that perhaps he wouldn't recognise me again, that perhaps someone like me would not be allowed to keep *any* child. So you see, Jonas . . . "

"Yes, yes," said Jonas.

92

"But his neck—the nape of a little boy's neck, have you ever noticed how touching it is, Jonas? It's probably the same with girls, but their's is hidden for the most part by their hair. But a little boy—" Lagerta's voice broke.

"If only I could forget," she said. "But of course you can't. And it's especially the nape of his neck I remember. From the moment he turned away from me and stood there for a little while looking at his presents, until he ran off. Sometimes I try to imagine the man he is now down there, grown up long ago, married perhaps and himself a father with little boys. All I can see is the nape of his neck, nothing but the nape of his neck—with that little dent in it . . . Besides, there's been another war since then."

And Lagerta burst into tears again, while Jonas, already at a loss, became even more embarrassed, although his expression hardened.

"Here I sit talking. What's the good of it? No-one can help me, no-one can change anything. And I had Gregor after all. Do you understand now, Jonas, what it meant to me to have Gregor?"

"Of course I do," said Jonas, but tonelessly. He got up and paced the floor again.

"My nerves are getting the better of me."

"Not surprising."

There was silence for a while, and then Lagerta said: "I became absurdly fond of Gregor, I *am* absurdly fond of him. What a word to use. Love can never be absurd. I want to see him happy, at peace with himself, but . . . I've tried with all my might to be fond of Dondi. Sometimes I actually was, and I thought that as long as we were really kind to her . . . But—"

Lagerta's anger returned. "To be honest I've almost—loathed her these last few years," she exploded. "I've fought against it as if it were a disease, or a vague, permanent feeling of sickness. I—simply didn't want to admit it. I thought it would help Gregor and the rest of us if I acted as if—as if . . . Today I don't seem able to see how it could have come about that he and Dondi— What do they really mean to each other?"

"Huh," said Jonas. "Gregor was lonely, and Dondi—"

"She was lonely too, Jonas."

"Dondi lonely? She was simply looking for someone to support her, and so, when the breadwinner didn't come up to expectations—"

"Oh Jonas, Jonas."

"It's not very pretty, I know, but believe you me, it's true. Dondi was skilled at looking deep into a man's eyes over the rim of her glass and—I imagine—at rousing his hopes. It's fairly widespread among Dondis and usually the only skill they possess. Many a good fellow has been taken in by a look full of promise over a glass. Then one day he's left feeling foolish and flat and empty with disappointment. Men seem to find that kind of woman particularly mysterious and attractive. The only mystery about it is that they want to be supported liberally without lifting a finger themselves."

"You talk as if you had had no end of bitter experiences, Jonas," said Lagerta, looking at him searchingly. "But Gregor wasn't an inexperienced boy either."

"Oh yes, he was. He's still as inexperienced as ever. I suppose it's part of his artistic make-up, his naiveté. How many times have we heard him say: 'Dondi isn't an ordinary woman'. By that he means she's quite exceptional, mysterious and exceptional. And he was cold, lonely and cold. And as you know, these chalets—"

"Yes, I suppose they're responsible for one thing and another. But since the two of us are talking about ourselves for once, Jonas," said Lagerta, who had so far composed herself that she now moved to the offensive. "You didn't answer me just now, you evaded the question as you have so many times before. I know I'm inquisitive, but I've taken your mother's place as best I could, and mothers are inquisitive. They can't resist it in the long run. And you have no idea how much I've wished, Jonas, wished more and more as the years have gone by, that you too would—I can't understand it, it seems to me you're so fitted for . . . "

Lagerta's courage failed her, and Jonas did not give her the slightest encouragement. He sat and looked at her without answering, glanced down at his hands folded loosely between his knees, looked up at her again. He swallowed, assuming a resolute expression, and Lagerta already regretted what she had said. Now she had gone too far, and she'd be scolded for it.

"You know what I mean," she said, somewhat accusingly.

"I know what you mean," said Jonas with unexpected calm, again looking away across the floor and then straight at her. "I've never been—really fond—of anyone but you," he said.

"Well, my dear, I hope you were fond of me. I did everything I could to win the confidence of my elder boy. But that's beside the point. Am I being terribly inquisitive, Jonas?"

"Yes, you are—inquisitive. But if you really want to know, you shall. I told you, I've never been really fond of anyone else but you."

"And I say I'm glad to hear it, Jonas. I had my doubts, especially at first. It was a long time before you showed any confidence in me. You were—reserved, perhaps? Nothing could make me happier than to know that you became really fond of me. But that that should prevent you from—I assure you, Jonas, no-one would have been more pleased than I. *You* wouldn't have found yourself a Dondi."

"Confound it, Lagerta, I 'doted' on you, as we used to say in the old days, when a man went about in love for years on end," exploded Jonas. "I know it's comic, laughable, what you will. But the fact is, you always came between me and the others, you were *always* there, I saw you and heard your voice. Many of them were beautiful and charming, splendid girls. But there you were—then as now, the prettiest, the most attractive, the—the quietest yet on occasion gayer than everyone else. Nothing was as good as your soft-spoken personality, there was nothing one longed to come home to more."

Lagerta stared at him in confusion as if seeing him for the first time. Then she recovered her composure and said: "Well—after all these years I suppose there's no harm in saying such a thing to an old woman well on in her fifties—your aunt into the bargain. Because that's what I am, however much you may protest. Think of it, your aunt. Now we can laugh about it, Jonas, laugh that you could ever have got such a silly notion into your head. That's all it was."

"If you mention the word 'aunt' again I'll—I'll get up and go. I won't stay here. 'After all these years' wasn't a very kind thing to say either. That wasn't like you. And is it 'harmless'?

"Who can tell what harm there is in putting long-suppressed feelings into words. Harm to oneself that is," he added in a low voice.

Lagerta again looked confused, and Jonas said: "Aunt? Aunt? Why did you keep harping on that all the time? Even today . . . "

"But I am your aunt," said Lagerta uncertainly, as if unable to defend her claim. "Your mother's sister who took your mother's place."

"You took Gregor's mother's place to such a degree that—"

"That what?"

"That you stayed on here—a lovely, charming woman one could so easily fall in love with. I don't mean you neglected me, you know that. You looked after me with all the care of which you were capable. If I discouraged you, it was because I was—shy of you, Lagerta."

"Very well, but you grew out of it, Jonas," said Lagerta with sudden determination. "From your feeling for me, I mean. I know that adolescent boys—"

"Rot. I wasn't the only one either. All the boys in my class doted on you. Before lessons began, if the teacher hadn't arrived, we all used to rush to the window when you went by. You were the prettiest and the best dressed and—I pretended not to care, but I was terribly proud of you."

And now Lagerta laughed aloud suddenly as if liberated: "And there was I, suspecting nothing. I *would* have put on airs if I'd known."

"You laughed then just as you used to in the old days," said Jonas.

"Ah yes, the old days." Lagerta became serious again and sighed, and Jonas hastened to say: "Sometimes someone would come courting you—visitors, and townsfolk who suddenly woke up and saw you properly for the first time."

"Did they?"

"Yes—and you never noticed. It seemed to go right over your head. So like you, Lagerta."

"You just imagined that, Jonas."

"Imagined it? Time and again I expected someone to make off with you. I was green with jealousy."

"A boy's fear of losing his mother again. The most natural thing in the world. I see how it was now."

"All you saw was Gregor. You were so taken up with Gregor when he was a child that you had no eye. for the rest of us. I don't suppose I'm the only man in love to have been jealous of a child."

"Good heavens," said Lagerta. "Jealous of your little brother?"

"Of him too, as I said. God knows why I'm going into all this."

Pause. Then Lagerta said with an effort: "I must admit I thought I noticed something, Jonas—maybe I did understand a little. On the other hand it was so preposterous, so incredible."

Jones lifted his head abruptly: "You understood, and you noticed? But you said nothing about it either? You're a great one for saying nothing, Lagerta."

"What would you have expected me to say? Saying nothing is the only weapon I have, it's my only means of defence. Besides, all of us say nothing in this house."

"What would I have expected you to say?" Jonas sat and thought about it for a little. "No, what could you have said? But did you have to defend yourself? Against a young nobody like me?"

"Don't misunderstand me, Jonas."

"No, of course not. You were sorry for me I suppose. I could never be anything more than a boy to you, naturally."

"In time you became the best friend I had," said Lagerta seriously. "You know that. And my dear— remember our ages. We were travelling on quite different trains," she said, attempting to joke a little. "When you began your journey, I had been on my way for a good many years already."

"Only a few years. Seven years. What's that, when you get down to it? What's seven years in a whole lifetime? The older you get the less it seems. I never thought it

98

mattered, it didn't affect me. I wasn't so foolish as to go round 'hoping', but since for once you asked me why my life is as it is, now you know."

"Listen, Jonas," said Lagerta earnestly. "There *were* young girls who—That nice girl who was staying at Dr. Berven's one summer, and several others. You *were* in love with her. For a long time I thought something would come of it. Then when she left and I heard nothing more, I realized that she wasn't going to be the one. But you mustn't say I've stood in your way. I won't have you saying you've been doting on an old woman like me. It's all so purposeless, so petty."

"It wasn't petty," said Jonas as if to himself. "Whatever it was, it wasn't petty. You weren't old all the time either. I know it doesn't conform to the usual pattern, but still—"

"I thought, Jonas," attempted Lagerta. "To tell you the truth I was afraid for you sometimes—afraid of your getting tied to the wrong woman and not getting free again. You're not the sort to run away from your obligations."

"What did you think? That I wasn't the soul of virtue? I never made myself out to be either. I'm only human. I suppose I wanted to—'forget' if possible, and—well, I was young. There was an affair with Auren the carpenter's daughter; she came home one summer and was very sweet. One with Oleanna Helgesen too—her mother sewed shrouds as you may remember. Fine, beautiful girls both of them. I kept them out of harm's way as long as I could, I didn't 'get them into trouble' as the saying goes. They've been married for many years now, the one in Sørfjord, the other in Skaafjord. They look plump and prosperous when they come to town occasionally. There were others too. I had my little adventures when I was out and about, like most young men. Little is the word

99

for them—they were quickly forgotten. But I'm surprised that someone should have gone to our respectable Lagerta with gossip of that kind."

"No-one did come and gossip. One gets to know things like that without hearing about them. Stop calling me respectable. Are you laughing at me?"

"Not on any account. But since you're pitching into me about the beautiful girls, I shall pitch into you about the dashing young men. What about young Consul Brun, when he came home from England? You were *very* impressed with him, Lagerta."

"Was I? Was *he* particularly dashing?"

"My word yes. And he courted you. I don't mind betting he proposed too before he went overseas again, the way he hung round here at all hours of the day, and all the flowers he sent you, and—There, look at you, blushing like a young girl."

"What nonsense, I'm not blushing, and he didn't propose. Besides, I didn't want to get tied up here. You can't do that if you're to hold out. It's easier to do things of your own accord than to be forced into them."

"That's true enough."

"But Jonas—" Lagerta's boldness had increased with his. "Why couldn't you have gone abroad and met her there? Don't you see, that's where you'd have found her. It was only because I came from the south that you were so infatuated with me."

"Yes," admitted Jonas. "People from the south do make an impression, if only for a while. But you—Good Lord, I admit I sometimes thought: Lagerta's getting on in years too. That was when you were tired and depressed. But scarcely were you out of sight when you appeared before me just as young as you used to be, young as no-one else ever had been, more beautiful than anyone else—richer in humanity, equipped with a kind of

100

halo. My step would become lighter just because I was on my way here, I hurried . . . The greatest stupidity of course, pure idiocy. And you were always up to something which made me love you even more, if it was only your helplessness, your childishness. You *are* helpless and childlike, Lagerta. You were the one I was most homesick for those years I spent being educated in Oslo and Hamburg. Who else should I have been homesick for, anyway? Gregor perhaps. Great-grandmamma, Grandmamma as we called her then. All due respect to Grandmamma, but she's not the sort of person you're homesick for."

Lagerta was in fact very moved as she listened to Jonas. But now she said in a commonplace tone of voice: "She's changed too."

"Yes, she has Dondi on the brain like the rest of us. It doesn't make you kind and gentle. You said I should have gone abroad. What about the firm? Should I have left it? With Øyen on the brink of the grave?"

"You wouldn't have gone for good. You'd have found yourself a wife and come home again. Although you might have stayed where you found her, too. Why not?"

"But my dear, what about you and the others?"

"There you are Jonas, who's sacrificing himself now? It's been you all the time!" exclaimed Lagerta. "I've often thought as much."

"Rubbish. If you had gone I might have come to my senses, especially if you had married. Although God knows—? But you stayed on here all those years, just as beautiful, just as charming, putting everyone else in the shade.

"But there," he drew it out. "Time changed things a little, I suppose."

"Yes, I'm sure it did, didn't it, Jonas?"

"I expect you would have left too, if Gregor hadn't

picked up Dondi. I can't fathom how you've never gone off the deep end sometimes up here."

"Oh, I have, on several occasions. But then I told myself that I was safe here, I had my hands full, nothing could—happen to me any more."

"Did the world seem as unsafe as all that?"

"The world *is* unsafe for people like me. We need something to anchor ourselves to."

"People like you. Are you going to start that again? God knows what you really mean by it?"

"Immoral women, that's what I mean."

"Now listen to me, Lagerta—"

"Immoral women. You've been doting on an immoral woman, Jonas. That's a good joke, isn't it?"

"Why do we have to drag everything into the mud?" said Jonas gently.

"I'm not dragging anything into the mud, I'm telling the truth. We're being so frightfully honest tonight. When 'respectable' people start being honest, the world really learns something new, as you see. Now consider me as the stranger I am."

"Don't be bitter, Lagerta. None of us had any idea how difficult things have been for you. We admired you for your generosity. If I had known what I know now, I for my part would have admired you even more."

"Imagine, admiration!"

"We loved you, we were grateful."

"I'm the one to be grateful. I was given the only thing that could have saved me, a child. Little by little I was able to look myself in the face again, although—" Lagerta was silent. "Besides, I had the right to protect myself as well as I could," she said, looking up defiantly.

"Naturally."

"So that I shouldn't be led into anything against my will any more."

"I repeat, you could surely have married and had children of your own?"

"You don't seem to understand anything, Jonas."

"No, perhaps not," said Jonas obediently.

"Supposing that, as well as everything else, I was so high and mighty that I didn't want to be dependent on anybody ever again."

"Didn't you become dependent on Gregor, then?"

"Yes, I did," said Lagerta, looking up again, astonished. "Yes, I did."

Jonas paced up and down. Lagerta was lost in thought. "Why should we two suddenly be talking so much about ourselves?" she asked after a while. "We're not concerned in all this."

"Doesn't it concern all of us?" replied Jonas. "Gregor stays here for Dondi's sake, and you for Gregor's sake. I —probably for both yours and Gregor's. At the bottom of everything we have Dondi."

"And what about the firm? The old firm?"

"Yes, I suppose so . . . "

Suddenly Lagerta started and listened, holding her breath. "Someone's coming. I heard the gate. It's Gregor."

Jonas halted at one of the windows: "Yes, here he is. I'll open the door so that he'll see us when he comes in."

"My God, how tired he looks," said Lagerta, also at the window. And she turned towards the open door as if expecting to see a ghost.

"Oh, he'll keep up appearances," said Jonas.

It was Gregor. With great care, he let himself almost noiselessly into the dim hall, and then stopped in front of the open living-room door as if he had come up against an unexpected trap. The light from inside fell directly on him. His face, which had been relaxed and tired, became stiff and impassive.

"Are you still up?" he said.

"As you see. Will you come in for a moment before you go upstairs? There are one or two things we must talk about."

"At this time of night? It's almost three o'clock."

"At this time of night."

"Dondi's waiting for me. She asked me to come home."

"We know that. Dondi's asleep."

"You can't possibly know *that*."

"Oh yes, we can. Come in and sit down."

"Thank you, I prefer to stand," said Gregor curtly. He came as far as the doorway, but no further. "Been sitting for hours in the boat," he said in explanation, clearly in order to take the edge off his curt tone of voice. "Had to be ferried across, of course. Not a bad idea in this weather though."

"Never mind about the weather, Gregor," said Jonas, equally curtly. And Lagerta felt the same anxiety she had occasionally experienced when they both were boys: Gregor, the 'gifted' one, the youngest by a good thirteen years, who has grown to be so much taller than his brother and distinguished himself in such different pursuits, the 'genius' of the family. Who is nevertheless so easily discouraged in many respects, in everyday matters. Who perhaps is no genius? Of course he is, as long as he gets the opportunity . . . He stood there in the unreal light between night and day—an illumination no less bright than the daylight, but different. He had an ungainly look about him, as he always did in his old sports clothes, in the windcheater which was too small and the shirt, anything but clean, which was open at the neck. He might have been a tramp. When he slung his knapsack off his shoulder a lock of hair fell over his forehead, and he so resembled himself as a boy that Lagerta was stabbed afresh with anxiety. It was a moment like so many other moments on such different occasions, and yet as if outside time. If she had dared, she would have gone over to him and taken his face in her hands as she used to long ago when something was really wrong. At the same time it struck her that he was handsome again, handsome in a new way. But tired. And afraid. I won't have him being tired and afraid, I won't have that dejected look that seems to have grown into his features during recent years; it never disappears completely, not even on the few occasions when he's cheerful. Surely Jonas isn't going to be hard on his little brother? Has he any right to be?

"You go to bed, Lagerta," said Jonas, who knew what she was thinking. "Try to rest a little while you can. The children will be off to school soon, if nothing else."

"They won't be going to school. The holidays began yesterday, Jonas."

"That too," said Jonas. "In other words we shall have them tearing in and out of the house. But go to bed, all the same. Thank you for keeping me company."

"Gregor must have some coffee."

"We can make the coffee ourselves," said Jonas, and his tone was such that Lagerta got up obediently and went. She looked grey and old in the morning light, her walk as she crossed the floor was that of an old woman, stiff and laborious. Both brothers watched her go.

"Take something to help you sleep if you have it," called Jonas after her. She nodded absently without replying.

Jonas paced up and down in silence for a while. Gregor observed him.

"Do you know why you're home?" asked Jonas eventually.

"I've no idea."

Jonas looked at him as if he found this difficult to

believe. "Dondi said she couldn't tell me over the phone," added Gregor.

"She's probably right about that. Look here, Gregor— I'm no diplomat—"

Jonas broke off and hesitated and Gregor shot in: "*You're* probably right about *that*."

"We're not schoolboys any longer, Gregor. You can save your sarcasm."

"Come along, out with it, Jonas. I can't stand here for ever. Dondi—"

"Oh Dondi. She's asleep."

"How can you know?"

"I know all right. We know when she's awake at any rate."

"Come to the point, Jonas."

"All right. Just one thing first. Hasn't it occurred to you that Lagerta will soon have had quite enough of you and your affairs and Dondi?"

"Has Lagerta complained about us?"

"You know very well she hasn't. When did Lagerta ever complain about anything? But hasn't it occurred to you that she's beginning to look as if you're plaguing her to death, both of you?"

"Aren't you a little confused, Jonas?" said Gregor.

"I'm not in the least confused. And you know very well what I mean."

"On the contrary," said Gregor curtly. His face was a mask, his eyes cold.

"Look here, Gregor, we've talked in riddles so long in this house that it's high time we spoke out. There's no time to beat about the bush, you'll soon know why. Dondi has succeeded in—but she'd better explain all that to you herself. What I want to say, before you go up to her and she starts singing any siren songs, is this: we'll put what money we can into a decent divorce if there's

106

any question of it, but not into one more of Dondi's whims. We've been so to speak—so to speak 'buying off' Dondi, time after time, at exorbitant rates. For your sake, for the sake of peace, so that Dondi should have something to keep her occupied, because—because that's how we are. Or rather, that's how Lagerta is, and Lagerta and 'we' amount to the same thing. But Dondi isn't our sort, she couldn't be more different. Dondi's the kind of person who destroys everything about her, material things and the goodwill of others. We've all known this for a long time, you too. Nobody expected that 'business' of hers to break even or to be a success, except perhaps Lagerta who's illiterate in such matters. I suppose we thought Dondi would soon get tired of it and that it could be liquidated without too great a loss. Now it's crashing round our ears, and we're going to let it crash as far as we're concerned. And *you're* going to let Dondi go while both of you are still at an age when you can hope to make a fresh start. It would be most fair to her too. One fine day it'll be too late."

Gregor struggled for words. He muttered: "So you've been cooking this up, all of you, while I was away."

"Not quite as quickly as that. Things have been—cooking—for a good while."

"Do you think I didn't know?"

At last he managed to find an answer. " 'Siren songs'," he said. " 'Whims'. What expressions! And as for 'buying off' Dondi, I never heard anything to equal it. Here I come home with no idea of what's the matter, and I'm hardly in at the door before you bombard me with insults against her and talk about God knows what—about divorce. Neither Dondi nor I want a divorce, as far as I'm aware."

"In that case you'll have to manage on your own from now on. And Dondi will have to put up with being a housewife, doing the housework, looking after her children—and—and behaving decently like other people. For it's no use putting on any more scenes, or floods of tears, or illnesses, or attacks. Even Lagerta isn't going to be impressed by all that any more, and we're not going to have it either. We want peace and quiet here. Dondi can't rise to that for two days at a stretch, and you know it."

Gregor made no reply to that. He had turned pale and drawn, and he fastened on to what Jonas had said previously, as if to an escape line. " 'Buying off Dondi'," he repeated indignantly. "You might consider what you're saying, Jonas."

"I have considered what I'm saying. I've considered long and thoroughly and often. The expression is disagreeable, I admit."

"And wrong. And unjust. 'Buying off Dondi'—As if her—her helpless attempts were—After all, the last thing she is, is *calculating*. But you've always looked down on her, all of you—you thought her—insignificant," said Gregor, taking refuge in something totally different.

"Far from it, Gregor. Insignificant? On the contrary, in her fashion significant. Dondi has calibre, she should have lived in America. There women of her type—and calibre—have real scope. There they have the word 'gold-digger' for people like her. It isn't a very attractive word in Norway either, and we don't gain much by paraphrasing it.

"If you knew how tired I was of all this beating about the bush, Gregor," exploded Jonas, and stopped pacing the floor for a moment. "There's been no end to it in this house. Great-grandmamma and myself are the only ones to have avoided it. We're the only individuals here with ordinary common sense. You and Lagerta—But of course you're both artists."

"Neither Lagerta nor I are artists, as you put it."

"Oh yes, you are, especially Lagerta. But she does all she can to ignore it, to forget it, that's my theory."

"Your theory, yes," said Gregor, not without scorn. " 'Gold-digger'!" he exclaimed, and concentrated on that. "Dondi a gold-digger? Anyone would think you didn't know the meaning of the word."

"If a rich man were to turn up, a man about town, you'd soon see the meaning of the word. Not that I think he will turn up now."

"You don't know what you're talking about, Jonas. Your stinginess simply makes you vulgar. I'm going. I can see something serious has happened, but I've no idea what. Oh—difficulties in the business, I suppose, but there are in so many businesses at the moment. It was Dondi who asked me to come home. I reserve the right to hear what she has to say first. You're simply attacking me by abusing her."

He turned at the door. "I understand how impatient you must get sometimes, Jonas, methodical as you are, good at figures, so different from the rest of us. Impatient with looking on, I mean, for *you* damn well didn't put any money into this. I get impatient myself now and again."

"You don't say? Yes, you have reason to be."

"But I'm—fond of Dondi, and—"

"Are you?"

"You have neither right nor reason to think otherwise. As for a divorce—I can't imagine ever letting her loose on her own, you know that perfectly well."

"There you let the cat out of the bag, my lad. Do you call that love? I thought you were supposed to be a psychologist," added Jonas.

"Call it what you like," said Gregor wearily. "It's a bond in any case, a devilish tight bond." And he went.

109

But Jonas called after him: "In all honesty, you must long to be free of this everlasting fuss and palaver?"

"People feel like that at times in all marriages, I suppose. If not there'd be nothing to it," said Gregor, pausing with his foot on the bottom stair.

"Then in God's name let the catastrophe come about, Gregor. Don't tell me the idea never entered your head. We haven't much time to spare. And were you—were you ever so very fond of Dondi? It's none of my business, but the way the situation—"

"God knows it's none of your business," said Gregor furiously, his face set. "Situation," he said. "You come talking to me about the situation. What situation? What sort of an attack is this, what sort of a conversation is it? From your point of view the situation has always been wrong. You can't stand Dondi, so everything to do with her is wrong. But now I'm going straight up to her, and—"

A door opened upstairs, an agonized voice called: "Are you never coming, Gregor?"

"Yes, of course, Dondi. I'm coming now."

There was a sob in reply, and Gregor patiently climbed the stairs.

Jonas watched him go. For an instant he shut his eyes as if he dared not let his feelings run away with him. When he opened them again his expression was calm and cold.

"There's only one thing to be done," he called after his brother.

No answer.

"Are you coming down again so that we can go on with our talk?"

"We'll see," came the curt reply. The door slammed.

110

V

Lagerta had not gone to bed. She remained sitting on the sofa in the dining-room, inert and paralysed, as people do when they will not take the trouble to lie down. She heard Jonas and Gregor behind the closed door, heard their voices rise and fall, become at times more heated, and drop even lower again. She heard Dondi call, and Gregor go upstairs, and Jonas leave the house quietly and cautiously. For a moment she thought of running after him, to learn more about their conversation, but could not summon sufficient energy.

And now the voice upstairs began in earnest, that voice which Lagerta thought she would be able to recognize many fathoms deep. Dondi had slept since mid-afternoon; she generally slept after Kaia had been in and out of the house. She ought to have been feeling groggy and perhaps she was, but she had remedies for that too, remedies which didn't make her any easier to deal with. Now her voice rose and fell, mounted to an hysterical soprano and descended to dramatic depths, leaving little room for Gregor's replies; replies that were brief and faint, and tired to such a degree that Lagerta felt it in her own body. Occasionally he interrupted violently, and Dondi would be quiet for a few moments.

"If only the walls weren't so thin," muttered Lagerta, for heaven knew which time in the course of the years. "But you can always hear everything in a villa, there's nothing to be done about it. Villas are all the same . . . "

Her paralysis seemed gradually to turn into a kind of mould into which she had stiffened; she had sat there for an eternity. She did not look up when the door opened cautiously and Karine came in, did not even start when the alarm clock in Karine's hand suddenly went off furiously. Only when Karine said to it angrily: "Hold your noise," stopping it roughly, did she jerk freezingly awake.

"So this is what it's come to, Miss Lagerta, poor thing! I've seen a lot of goings-on in this house, but not even going to bed, that beats everything. Master Jonas ought to hear of it, and the old lady, so they could put matters to rights up here. My word, wouldn't they be scandalized!"

Unspeakably scandalized herself, Karine shook out pillows and blankets and forced Lagerta to lie down. Patient, compliant, chilled to the bone, Lagerta submitted to her scolding, only muttering: "It doesn't happen very often, Karine."

A little later she accepted hot coffee without protest, the American coffee which Karine had used without asking permission, and whose aroma drifted deliciously in from the kitchen. Lagerta drank it eagerly, saying nothing, seeming not to give a thought to her surroundings. She ate quickly and greedily, as hungry as she used to be in her childhood after a ski trip. Only afterwards did she look up and smile her thanks at Karine.

"Serve you right if I went straight to our Jonas," was Karine's final shot, but her voice had relented. "I ought to undress you like the baby you are," she muttered, as she tucked the blanket tightly round Lagerta's freezing shoulders. "It won't be a long rest, but you make the best of it. When they've talked themselves to a standstill up there they'll come down here with their noise, I know all about it. By that time I'll have a bath ready for you, Miss Lagerta, and I'll thank you to take it, too."

"If I have time, Karine."

"Time? I'll thank you to make time, Miss Lagerta." With which Karine departed.

Lagerta may have slept in snatches, but she kept waking up, disturbed by a door shutting somewhere, by a bed creaking upstairs, by the voice overhead that still rose and fell, but more evenly now, whimpering as if overpowered, and finally falling silent.

She tried to think, small short sequences which soon petered out, muttering them to herself as was her habit. "The children will sleep late. Heaven knows what time they came home last night—we shall have to get them and their music out of the way later on so that the rest of us can talk . . . We must . . . Jonas said it was urgent . . .

"He'll have to see to it," she went on muttering. "He and Karine . . . Food in the kitchen and scolding . . . But he mustn't scold Gregor. Things are bad enough for Gregor as it is . . .

"What was all that Jonas was talking about just now? A lot of childish, silly nonsense, schoolboy nonsense that should have been forgotten long ago. Perhaps he dragged it up out of sympathy—yet, of course, sympathy—to make himself seem a bit miserable too. After all, I was turning myself inside out. What on earth did I want to do that for? I've never behaved so foolishly . . . All that suffering that's now so far behind me, I seem to be looking at it through the wrong end of a telescope—why should I have brought it up? It was a heavy responsibility of course, but such an old one that at last it seemed to have fallen away from me into a deep chasm. Events may have uncovered it again, but more and more seldom . . . And now, a generation later, it comes flooding back so violently that it deprives me of my will. Of being able to hold my tongue, which is only proper, the only way to keep up appearances. Those things shouldn't be told to other people, you simply have to put up with them—admit your responsibility and put up with them—irreparably distressing and shameful as it is. As for trying to make amends for the wrong you've done—as if amends could be made for anything like that. A lot of nonsense this new gospel preaches—as long as everything's brought out into the open it'll be all right. It isn't all right, and you only become more contemptible. A person must have a little dignity . . . I suppose I thought I had achieved some . . . Now I find I've even failed myself.

"It's a good thing Jonas is a man, at any rate. He'll understand just enough of it to understand nothing at all. Women understand too little and too much; they either sit in judgment or get sentimental . . . 'Sympathetic' females—eyes brimming with tears and laying on of hands . . . dear, oh dear, oh dear . . .

"Have I no patience with my own sex any more?" muttered Lagerta. "Evidently not. Great-grandmamma's all right, though. She's edgy and difficult, often irritating, but never clinging, never indiscreet. Nor is Karine. What a blessing that the two women with whom I spend most time should be as they are—dry—dry and healthy, like— like well-baked, slightly stale bread . . . Gracious me, if I'm not lying here getting literary too . . .

"Not today, Great-grandmamma, it's not convenient today. You're not bound to turn up because you said you would, but you may suddenly stand there thumping your stick . . . Or sit there with your knitting . . . Not today, Great-grandmamma—"

At this point Lagerta heard her own voice and stopped, disconcerted. "Old woman!" she said to herself firmly, shut her mouth tight, and lay looking up at the ceiling. She was not certain whether it was a dream or reality when she saw Jonas peering cautiously round the door. "Jonas," she called, as if to test her dream. And he opened the door wide and was real after all.

"Thought I'd better look in. Good heavens, haven't you even undressed?"

"There's some coffee over there, Jonas, good coffee. Ask Karine to warm it up."

114

But Jonas poured out the coffee as it was, drank it quickly and eagerly and devoured the remains of the food. It disappeared in two mouthfuls and Lagerta cried, shocked: "You haven't eaten a thing today."

"No, as a matter of fact I haven't. That was good. Don't send for Karine now, somebody's coming downstairs."

There was a knock on the door. Jonas opened it. It was Gregor.

"Are *you* here?" he said. "You're up early. That's all to the good, I want to talk to you too."

"You want to talk to me *first*. Now go to bed properly, Lagerta, get undressed and sleep until afternoon. We'll wake you if necessary. You're up early too, I must say, Gregor."

"I came down to talk to Lagerta," protested Gregor. "It won't take long," he added; and Lagerta had already thrown aside the blanket so as to get up, when Karine appeared in the kitchen doorway accompanied by a distant sound of running water, to announce firmly: "Your bath water's hot now, the tub's nearly full. It'll rest you. Come along, Miss Lagerta. Our Gregor can wait a little, can't he now?"

With which she led Lagerta as if under arrest towards the noise of the water, and Lagerta suddenly gave in and went obediently, only pausing to say: "Promise me you'll give Gregor coffee, Karine. He had none last night."

"Of course, they shall all have coffee. We've been drinking coffee non-stop ever since yesterday. There'll soon be an end of the little we've got. But he shall have coffee, he shall certainly have his coffee. Just you come along."

In the living-room the brothers remained standing

each in front of a window. Their faces worn and tired, they both stood looking out; at the sun in its normal daytime position shining on the slopes of the mountain, and at the fishing smack which chugged down the fjord leaving a long glittering stripe behind it. The fine weather would hold.

Something snapped inside Gregor, a growing feeling of exasperation, of resentment. He swallowed, tight-lipped, and was about to say something, but Jonas was the first to break the silence. "It can't be very easy for you living with us all the time, Gregor?"

"Easy?" said Gregor, surprised. "It's hell," he said, involuntarily. "But I suppose I have no right to think so. And what can you know about it, Jonas?

"It'll come to an end some time, I suppose," he muttered non-committally, half to himself, as if to gloss over what he had said.

"I *try* to understand," said Jonas. "I'm just a provincial, but—"

"You've been abroad."

"As a tourist, yes."

"You studied commerce."

"In Hamburg. I loathed Hamburg and the family I lived with and everything about it. I don't count that. But let's get back to you—of course you have the right to think it's hell. I'm glad to hear you say so. Now do let's be frank for once in a while. Did you get Dondi to tell you what all this is about?"

"Dondi isn't fit to give an account of anything at the moment. There can't be so much haste, surely. She's exhausted with insomnia and—"

"And with poison and devilry. But never mind, we'll manage without her, much better in fact. It'll save us a lot of bother. No haste, did you say? Oh yes, Gregor, but there is."

"You might be a little reasonable, Jonas, and give her time to come out with what she has to say. She's seeing to something that'll solve the whole problem, she says, if only we'll all wait a little and have a bit of patience. That fellow Andersen is pestering the life out of her."

"He's pestering about money."

"Obviously, I realize that. I said long ago that Dondi knew nothing about running a business. But Lagerta was so enthusiastic about the idea, and—"

"Oho, so the blame is to be put on Lagerta?"

"No, no, of course not, but Dondi must be allowed to have her say as well. She will, she says, as soon as she's collected her wits and seen to—seen to whatever it is she's doing. Surely you can give her a *little* respite? She got hold of a powder again, she asked for it."

"To sleep through her difficulties. We know that trick of old. And Dondi's going to 'see to' something. *Are* you stupid, Gregor, or do you make yourself seem so?"

"Oh, I'm stupid all right," said Gregor tamely, sighing with weariness.

Jonas glanced at him, and his own face relaxed with exhaustion for a moment, but he stiffened again. "I'm afraid you are. Very much so where certain matters are concerned. We were going to talk about you anyway."

"Me?"

"Yes, you. You have no ambition, Gregor."

"What has my ambition to do with it? We're discussing Dondi and Dondi's business. I realize you're all at the end of your tether—"

"You are not ambitious *enough*," insisted Jonas.

"Ambitious, ambitious," repeated Gregor in irritation. "I'm as ambitious as the devil. What do you know about it, the lot of you?"

"Very little in recent years, it's true. But you *appear* unambitious."

"Unambitious? On the contrary I'm probably so arrogant that neither praise nor censure can affect me any more. But what has this got to do with it?"

"That sort of arrogance isn't new by any means. And I believe it does have something to do with it. Never mind about praise and censure; what about the real triumphs?"

"I don't know. I've never had any."

"Don't you consider your first book to have been a considerable triumph?"

"If we must talk about this, a triumph is surely a kind of inner experience which can't be described, in words or in writing. A great deal happened at that time as you may know. I had no time to think about the book at all. What do you want to go into all this for, Jonas? I have the right to be spared it."

"We must go into a number of things," said Jonas. "For once we must try to see matters as they are, however distressing it may be. I realize you didn't have time to think much about the book then. But you must have been pleased with your success, it must have caught up with you later. If nothing else, you had friends whose opinion you valued."

"One's friends," said Gregor quietly. "They don't understand much. I don't want to offend you, Jonas, but a friend, even if he's one's brother . . . "

"All the better if a brother can be counted as a friend. Listen Gregor, there's one thing we friends who are your brothers, and certainly those friends who are not, will never be able to understand. That you don't break out."

"Against what?" said Gregor sharply. His eyes were watchful.

"Against everything. Against your life here."

"Are you back on the subject of my marriage to Dondi?"

118

"That too. You're not happy, Gregor."

"Happy? Who is? But it's wrong to put all the blame on Dondi."

"No-one puts all the blame on her."

"The blame, Jonas, rests with the circumstances and a good many other things. To take the one nearest home—myself. I'm a heretic as you know, I don't subscribe to authority. I don't believe people can be classified and listed and judged according to doctrine. Very simple people maybe, primitives, those lacking complexity of any kind—to a certain extent the sick."

"And the second one?" asked Jonas expectantly.

"The second one, what second one? I came down to discuss Dondi's business with Lagerta, not you. To find out whether anything can be done about it. Then you arrive on the scene and suggest I get a divorce! Even if I were able to meet the expense—and even if Dondi were able to contribute the smallest amount towards her upkeep . . . I don't mind admitting that when she started her hairdresser's shop I thought, perhaps this is the beginning of—"

"The end?" interrupted Jonas with a hint of scorn in his voice.

"Of something new," Gregor corrected him harshly. "Something better for her and for me—for all of us."

"What do you really *feel* for Dondi? You can't possibly be anything but fed up with her, thoroughly fed up."

"What do I feel? Something very complex, sometimes one thing, sometimes another. My feelings are divided, I suppose. But affection predominates. I imagine I'm fond of her really?"

"You felt differently towards Harriet?"

Gregor looked distressed. "They're so dissimilar," he said. "You can't compare things like that. You ask the

119

most absurd questions. And without justification. What right have you to ask such a thing?"

"No right at all. Forget it."

"What do you know about feelings, anyway," said Gregor aggressively.

"I've never taken a diploma in them. But you find quiet, self-taught people in all fields of knowledge. Nobody takes much notice of them. Then all of a sudden it appears that they've learnt something, all on their own."

"What nonsense," said Gregor angrily. But he stopped short and said: "You asked me last night what bound me to Dondi. I told you that I was responsible for her, responsible for her and the children. It's simple enough."

"You're responsible for yourself too," said Jonas unmoved.

Gregor did not reply.

"An unhappy person for whom I am responsible," he said with emphasis after a moment's thought.

"Nobody wants you to leave her to fend for herself."

"If Dondi were left on her own it would amount to the same thing. Do you know what sympathy is, Jonas? Oh no, you don't. You're the type with everything in order, a pattern of virtue, a—"

"That'll do, Gregor."

"And the children," said Gregor. "What about the children?"

"Those terrible youngsters."

"Yes, they are terrible. That's not their fault, it's due to circumstances too. I readily admit I can't manage them."

"You can't even manage to control yourself. You're so obviously impatient with them, let alone downright irritable."

"Good Lord, Jonas, give me a little time," said Gregor, helpless all of a sudden. "I intend to deal with it, I—"

"You'll never be able to deal with anything as things are now, you knew that long ago. You behave like Dondi's slave. Or rather, your own slave. You live enslaved by outmoded superstition."

"Perhaps so," said Gregor wearily.

"You're 'bourgeois', Gregor."

"If it's bourgeois to look after one's own affairs and to try to do the right thing as far as possible, then I'm very bourgeois. I've never set myself up to be a Bohemian."

"No, it's true you don't waste your time down at the Grand at night with the couple of fellows in this town who think they are. You don't wear odd clothes, you—"

"I wander about the roads a good deal when other people are sitting over their book-keeping and accounts. That's rather un-bourgeois, isn't it?" said Gregor sarcastically.

"You wander about, yes. Do you get anything out of it?"

Gregor sighed despondently. "Sometimes, sometimes not. You're asking absurd questions again. One must sit at a desk as well, you know."

"That's when the cottage should come in handy."

"It does."

"When you're allowed to go there, you should have said."

"But of course I am."

Jonas opened his mouth to reply, but closed it again, at a loss for words perhaps, or out of charitableness. Gregor said in a preoccupied way, as if talking to himself: "Those timeless interludes—when there's no difference between day and night—when you eat what you happen to have, when you happen to feel like it—and the rest of the world ceases to exist. You do get through to them, if you get the chance to wander about for a while. Something materializes inside you, something at least *partly* usable. But then the world breaks in. It doesn't go with family life, that sort of thing."

"Not with Dondi at any rate."

"Not with anyone. I don't know that Dondi's worse than anybody else in that respect."

"You know very well she is."

"*All* one's surroundings are more or less appalling," said Gregor curtly.

"Dondi more so."

"I don't know about that."

"Oh yes, you do. Dondi can't even be bargained with."

"Bargained with?" said Gregor, but was interrupted by a knock on the door. It opened, and in marched Karine. "Coffee for Gregor," she announced ungraciously, put the tray down with a clatter, and went out again. Gregor poured it out and drank it nervously and with appetite, then took a few bites of food while Jonas silently looked the other way, as if allowing an opponent a moment's truce for water. He jingled his keys impatiently in his trouser pocket.

Gregor put down the food and wiped his mouth. "Bargained with?" he repeated, as if the word in itself implied something unprecedented. "Having to bargain at all is intolerable. The whole world wants to be bargained with. You have to keep the world informed, explain yourself, *excuse* yourself to the world. 'But of course I understand you must have quiet,' it is said as soon as the world is in the know. Then everyone goes on tip toe, closing doors quietly, and whispering at the top of his voice. That's precisely what's so damned impossible, 'bargaining' for peace and quiet. You give up, it paralyses you. People who really get things done obviously have the capacity for not giving a damn about their surroundings, for letting everything go to the devil, it must be so. All right, I know I'm impossible. And ungrateful. And that everything is being done for me, and—"

"But I'm quite resigned really, let me tell you," stated Gregor in a new tone of voice, looking at Jonas as if to confirm what he was saying.

"You're self-controlled, much too self-controlled."

"Self-controlled? No. Submissive, cowed. Done for probably."

"Not yet. But it mustn't be allowed to go any further."

Gregor shrugged his shoulders, as if the assertion were sheer nonsense. "Earlier today you were talking about 'buying off'. That's what a writer is forced to do, it seems to me. You never know yourself where your subject-matter will lead you. But the world wants to know about it. The world wants to be in the know. So that it can boast of its knowledge."

"I've not asked you about your work, Gregor. I've known since we were boys that I shouldn't do that. Neither Lagerta nor I have pestered you, nor has Great-grandmamma. I hope you're aware that you're saying all this unprovoked. It doesn't strike home as far as we're concerned."

" 'Unprovoked'," repeated Gregor bitterly. "That's a good one. I'm saying it so as to throw a bone to the world. The world always wants a bone to gnaw, it waits constantly for one. Never asks, just watches and waits. You too, Jonas, you too, whether you realize it or not. Oh yes—we buy ourselves off, we too. You introduced this subject, not I."

"I was talking about your working conditions, not your work. You're tired, and you misinterpret everything. It may not be so easy to belong to the world all the time either, Gregor."

"Good Lord, do you think I don't realize that? I exist here like a criminal, I—"

"As a representative of this insufferable outside world, I'm going to ask you a question you won't like," interrupted Jonas with decision. "Isn't it difficult for you to find any material in the humdrum life you lead here? Humdrum, and yet so restless."

"Material? Can you complain about that? I measure out my material like an industrious moth, I hoard every scrap. I walk and walk, and out comes one short story after another. Ten pages in double spacing, neither more nor less. Just the right size, suitable for a weekly. Machine-trimmed—good for its purpose—"

"And then you collect them into some sort of book," said Jonas lightly, as if *en passant*.

" Exactly. Which occasionally turns out to be a regular disgrace to the family. A sizeable fiasco."

"You were rapped over the knuckles by one or two of the critics last time, and there wasn't much sale. That can happen to the best writers. And one day you'll make a come-back with—with something different."

"Come-back," said Gregor, in torture, though he, too, spoke as if the matter was of no importance. "That's a good one too. I've got a pile of papers lying there, a shapeless mass of material. You can correct and add and strike out, and it's still just as far from being finished. No, Jonas..."

"Come, come, Gregor."

"This perpetual obligation to produce something 'of importance' again."

"Obligation?"

"Yes, obligation. To the publisher and you and Lagerta and Dondi and the children and God and the whole wide world. If I start thinking about it, it stifles me. So I 'collect' a few stories again. Heaven knows it was far better to be young and 'unnoticed'. But I got myself into this."

"Here in the north you're unnoticed," said Jonas, his tone of voice implying that now it was his turn.

"Yes, and it's the only bright spot as far as I'm concerned. I know it costs money, I know I ought to wish it were otherwise, but without it I'd be entirely without hope. The short time I was 'noticed' I had more than enough. For an author, to be noticed means having everybody trying to scrape up an acquaintance with you. Some of them think you're an oracle whose words of wisdom will solve their problems if only they can bare their souls to you. Some of them simply want to wear you in their buttonholes, say they know you, at the very worst give parties on the strength of your reputation. 'So and so, the author, has promised to come.' "

"I seem to remember your being pleased at receiving a letter," interrupted Jonas.

"Perhaps I was green and naïve enough to be pleased. Sometimes you even write a few words of thanks in reply. If your luck's out you get twelve pages back again. You have to pay for being a somebody."

Gregor's voice choked suddenly, he forced out his words: "" I'd like to tell them to their faces that I hate writing, that I curse the day I began to write. Or rather, the day I let myself be taken in by fine words and *went on* with it, instead of taking up something better while there was still time. One book proves nothing. That old poet was perfectly right to oppose my getting a government award on the basis of my first book. The second book was a fiasco. And every book since has been a fiasco."

"Some of the stories—" said Jonas.

"Yes, they're supposed to show evidence still of 'a certain fine talent' here and there. 'Much is still expected of me', was the gracious conclusion of one poor review. When is he going to 'give us' something again, as it was put even more prettily. It turns up in the letters too, it's a popular catchphrase. 'Giving'—imagine it. Anything we produce that's any good has been tortured out of us. Those are screams lying on the Christmas book-shelf, stitched and bound. That's what they want, screams. But I have no right to complain. Why am I not an office clerk? Or working for you on the wharf? I might not have been too bad at it?"

"Heaven preserve me from having you on the wharf," said Jonas. "It's the way you live that makes you feel like this, Gregor. And yet you never say a word."

"What's the use? Everyone has to live under certain conditions, doesn't he? Burdens that have been assumed, and can't be rejected out of hand, not by anyone with decency. You may have a family, for instance, and you're incapable of doing anything besides this wretched scribbling. And you're not even any good at that either ... Don't ask about anything more, Jonas. There are questions everyone thinks he has the right to ask, especially if he's given you any help. I don't mean Lagerta, she never asks about anything. But others, publishers and such like, one's few 'friends', even one's brother, apparently. Oh yes, Jonas. And naïve, outspoken readers—a letter still trickles in occasionally. All because you write. If you made sausages, you'd be left in peace. I hate the whole business, I could vomit. There was Dondi as well of course. She was mighty active when we were in Oslo. With the best of intentions, naturally."

"All meddling is done with the best of intentions," said Jonas curtly. "And persons 'in love', as they so strangely put it, insist in nine cases out of ten on changing the object of their affections so that he fits in with *their* pattern, solves *their* problems. I've seen quite a bit of that. Dondi's activity."

"It was hard on Dondi. In the end she hung about

Grand Hotel and the Theatre Café morning, noon and night. The trouble was she didn't cut any ice with the right clique. After all, she's no intellectual. She was ignored in spite of her beauty. That was before she got the unfortunate notion of dying her hair."

"I can just see her sitting there, one leg crossed over the other, a cigarette, and a few drops of vermouth in the bottom of her glass."

"Very possible. How do you know?"

"That's how they do sit. I made my observations too, you know, when I went south once in a while."

"Damn you and your observations. All right, I'm sorry, but—Dondi was elbowed aside, and ended up amongst the others who waited with the same hope of becoming accepted. She hoped for so much that never came to anything . . . I was to meet all sorts of people, I was to read the gospel for the day. As I said, she meant well."

"When has Dondi not meant well? If there's anyone who thinks of what's best for others—"

"Jonas! She did mean well, she believed in it all. She wasn't alone in that. It's a sphere for the intelligent, and I'm hopelessly old-fashioned and naïve myself. But it was beyond Dondi's scope."

"It's supposed to be within everybody's scope these days, Dondi's too," remarked Jonas.

"Maybe so. But damn it all, this is off the point. Dondi's business—"

"We're coming to that. Just one question first. It is true about this girl who comes and goes at the cottage?"

Gregor looked surprised for an instant. Then he said: "Comes and goes is a slight exaggeration. She's been there a few times."

"I know it's very indiscreet to ask, but—can you see her taking Dondi's place?"

"Taking Dondi's place? They couldn't be more

different." Gregor was obviously searching for something to prevent further indiscretion on Jonas's part, but Jonas was too quick for him. "Good. We couldn't put up with another Dondi in the family."

"Oh, there'll be no question of family relationships. In my position I can't drag anyone else into my life."

"It seems to me you've already done so," said Jonas dryly. "You know what it's like in a small town like this. Why don't you go away for a while, Gregor?"

"I'd rather not at the moment," said Gregor quietly. "For several reasons."

"Take her with you."

"She's not the kind of girl you take with you. And what about Dondi? I couldn't spring anything like that on her."

"Of course you could—well, never mind. In that case both of you should be above staying here to be gossiped about. There will be gossip, there is already, it has reached me as you see. Go away, Gregor, go away for a time, and go alone, that would be best. Get everything into perspective from a distance. Go to Paris. I'll help you as far as I can. It won't be very much, we're scraping the bottom of the barrel."

"Thank you, I can well imagine it, if you have any say in the matter. And Paris? Why Paris?"

"Because that's where you really lived once, if only for a short time," said Jonas, ignoring Gregor's comment. "I can imagine it might be a kind of—rebirth—for you. Besides, where else does one go?"

But Gregor's expression closed up even more. "A pretty thought. But I can't do any of it. I can't go to Paris and I can't leave Dondi. And what would I do in Paris? Move from hotel to hotel like a refugee? You can't find anywhere to stay there for long these days, unless you have lodgings already."

"Dondi will manage," said Jonas.

"Dondi manage! No-one can get herself into a muddle quicker than Dondi. She's too frail."

"Frail? Dondi? She's as strong as a horse, stronger than any of us."

Gregor made no reply. He said: "None of you remember what it meant for Dondi to have to come north. She's a southerner. Up here it takes a great deal to—"

"It takes love, I imagine," said Jonas curtly.

"And are you implying that Dondi is incapable of it?"

"I've never come across anybody who lacked it more. She has no idea what it means. And as for you, you're—"

"A fool, I suppose."

"Something of the sort, yes."

"Thank you."

"One fine day you may thank me in a less ironical tone of voice. You were never in love with Dondi, were you Gregor?"

"Damn you for your persistence," said Gregor in exasperation. "I don't have to account to you for my feelings, do I? What do you understand about such things? I—I longed for human contact, to be in somebody's arms, somebody I could have affection for and who would have affection for me. Somebody whose hand I could hold when life was bad—and when it was good too. I was damnably alone—a dog without a master. We'd just about had enough, Dondi and I. So I thought that—"

"All that's very reasonable, Gregor."

"I didn't expect to 'fall in love' any more. We were both aware that there was no romance about it. We simply wanted to help each other."

"Yes, oh yes."

"What do you mean by 'oh yes'?"

"That it was certainly true as regards yourself."

"And as regards Dondi. We discussed it frankly. But

in the long run Dondi doesn't seem to be able to manage . . ."

"You can't manage it either. You can't manage any of the things Dondi expects of you."

"I can't manage anything anyone expects of me."

"You're not the pushing type."

"No, nor is Dondi."

"On the contrary, that's exactly what she is. Two pushing together may get what they want, but never one who's pushing and one who isn't."

"Dondi pushing?" said Gregor.

"A calculating pusher. One of the most calculating I've ever come across."

"Look, it's time this conversation came to an end. It's gone too far, not once, but over and over again."

Gregor started towards the door, but stopped halfway as if about to say something else.

"It's about time conversations in this house did go too far," said Jonas after him.

"You talk about love," said Gregor. "Falling in love. I wasn't in love. Do you realize what an obligation that is? I was lonely and unhappy. Dondi was lonely and unhappy. If you must know, I was weak enough to seduce Dondi. I have all kinds of obligations towards her. I'm telling you this because you're my brother, because you've been helpful in your fashion, although you were against us most of the time. Help has to be paid for."

"Now don't be bitter," said Jonas. "So you think you seduced Dondi? No fear, Dondi seduced you. It's always Dondi and her type who do the seducing. I know enough about women to be able to work that one out."

"Working it out as usual! For once you've worked it out wrong."

"I don't think so. It's never amusing for a man to be seduced."

"How can you be so vulgar, Jonas?"

"We shall have to discuss it sooner or later," said Jonas, unruffled. "We shan't be through with Dondi unless we do. I remember it well, as a matter of fact. It was obvious that Dondi wanted you far more than you wanted her. You were uncertain of yourself."

"Is my responsibility any the less for that?"

"She more or less put herself to bed with you at the chalet. Poor little innocent Dondi."

"Dondi never made herself out to be innocent. She came from circles which—you know all about that, Jonas. Dondi has been through a great deal. Two ship-wrecked survivors can help each other—I suppose I thought something of that sort when I let myself be 'seduced' as you so prettily put it. To me there was something pathetic about Dondi which appealed for protection. There still is, call her a 'gold-digger' as much as you like. I knew you were stingy, but it's not like you to be so small-minded, Jonas."

"I'm not saying we shouldn't 'protect' Dondi as far as we can," said Jonas, still unruffled. "But we must protect you as well. It's high time, the years are passing. You'll never break away on your own."

Gregor was not listening. His vexation at the expression 'gold-digger' blazed up again. "If it weren't so ugly it would be comic. In the first place a gold-digger wouldn't marry a struggling young author."

"Oh yes, she would," said Jonas. "A rather naïve gold-digger. They have odd ideas about authors and their incomes. Like other honest folk, they consult the publishing figures in the newspapers, calculate so much per copy, and conclude that this is a lot of easily earned money. I've heard that kind of argument."

"Gold-digger! What a simplification."

"Simplification is occasionally necessary, but in any case this is no simplification."

"Why did you say 'we'? 'We must protect you as well'. Does that mean you and Great-grandmamma?"

"Lagerta too perhaps."

"Lagerta? Never. What hasn't she done for Dondi, precisely for Dondi? If anyone has been on Dondi's side in this house, it's Lagerta. She's more than patient with Dondi, she's fond of her."

"Do you really believe that, Gregor?"

"No," said Gregor dejectedly. "No, I know everyone's fed up. Even Lagerta's feelings are beginning to wear thin."

"And your own?"

"Good Lord, mine? Have I any right to be fed up? I must put up with my responsibilities. You set a trap for me there, Jonas."

"Lagerta has been a simple believer," said Jonas, ignoring his reference to traps. "But doubts can afflict the believer too, and I think they're afflicting her. But she hasn't said anything yet, it's true."

"I thought as much. However fed up Lagerta may be, she's still on our side."

"Eternally on *your* side, Gregor. Now why don't you go upstairs and rest too, and then perhaps it'll be possible to talk to you properly. What did you want to come down so early for? To worry Lagerta? To pester her? To extort more money out of her? She must be left in peace until lunch time at least. After that we shall have to come to a decision. Dondi has driven the business past saving on to the rocks, and there it must lie. Then there's the future to be settled."

"I wish to goodness you'd stick to the business, Jonas. I realize something's wrong with it, I never had much faith in it anyway. But why should we get a divorce?

132

Dondi doesn't want a divorce any more than I do."

"That's possible. She can't prevent it."

"Of course she can. She has her rights too. You only see Dondi's failures, not her—pathetic—little attempts to help, to be of some use."

"Use? Has there been one occasion on which you've been left in peace at your cottage? Has she been of as much use as that?"

"Of course she has. Lord, I wonder if I could go back again tonight, Jonas. It *has* happened before."

"I don't see why not. Sometimes when I read your books, Gregor, the ones that sell as well as the ones that don't, I think: He has an eye for people. But where Dondi's concerned you're as blind as a bat."

"And what do you have an eye for? Money, money, money. No Jonas, I don't mean you have an eye for money exclusively, but if anyone's blind where Dondi's concerned, it's you. You refuse to see any good side to her character at all. In my eyes—"

"—'she's quite out of the ordinary', I know. That's obvious. Someone whom you allow to keep you in order and for whom you sacrifice everything shouldn't be too insignificant. And you're supposed to be a psychologist? And a poet? I'm darned if we businessmen aren't better psychologists. You authors recreate people until they resemble the dream you live in. We don't suffer from that weakness."

"No, what are your weaknesses? You have none, for then you couldn't be businessmen. Have you any idea what a *bond* sympathy is? It's the toughest of them all. Once you're bound by it . . . Imagine suggesting a divorce to me before I've so much as mentioned it to Dondi."

"I want to make it clear to you where the rest of us stand, *before* you go up to talk to her. If you and she intend to stay together you'll have to manage on your own from now on. There's nothing extraordinary going on here today; all this is quite normal, only on a grander scale than usual. If I don't speak my mind everything will develop normally too. Dondi cries. Dondi rings up Lagerta and cries. We've got as far as that stage of the proceedings already. Dondi talks you into selling the cottage and the car."

"The cottage *and* the car?"

"This time it's a matter of both. When we get to the cottage, if not before, Lagerta says: 'Don't cry, Dondi, I'll see to it.' Because giving up the cottage is tantamount to giving up you, to giving up all hope of seeing you gain recognition as an author. Lagerta writes a cheque as usual. It will be the last one she'll ever write, and it'll cause her embarrassment because she can't honour it."

"She knows best about that. And you're forgetting something. I do work."

"When you get tranquillity you do. You need tranquillity for a long period of time, Gregor, in order to find yourself again, if I may put it that way. And tranquillity means freedom from Dondi, a long period of freedom from Dondi. Lifelong freedom, if it's to be any good at all."

"And you think that would mean tranquillity? If only it were so simple. There's too much you people don't understand, or even begin to know about."

"That may be so. But I do know and understand about one thing. You two are not going to extort any more money out of Lagerta. I know it's not you, it's never you. Even so, it must come to an end."

"The way you put things! Anyone would think we owed money to you, but it happens to be Lagerta. Yes, I know you're involved as well, we live here, we eat here at your expense every day, I realize you keep accounts. It's

134

no use talking to each other, Jonas," said Gregor, making as if to go again.

"After all, Lagerta's quite well off," he said, turning. "That old uncle left her everything he had. It was quite a packet."

"In those days it was. Lagerta used to be well off. She isn't any longer."

"Good Lord, she gave the children jazz instruments the other day, expensive ones. Surely she wouldn't have done that if—?"

"And you think that because Lagerta gives expensive presents, Lagerta is rich? You've lived in the same house with her year after year, as a child and a grown man, and you still don't know any better than that? Lagerta is the world's worst spendthrift. If she's fond of someone she throws money around without a thought for what she does or doesn't have. She has no idea what she has, in any case. Lagerta's an imbecile where financial matters are concerned. You ought to know that, but of course it may often be more convenient—and easier—to turn a blind eye to it."

"You disgust me, Jonas. Thank God I don't owe you any money."

"Are you quite sure you don't?"

"I ought to be sure, apart from the food and lodging, and I'll pay that back again one of these days. The rest is a matter between Lagerta and myself."

"That's how it may look," said Jonas quietly, standing as usual at one of the windows.

"You really are irritating, Jonas. Are you Lagerta's keeper?"

"No," said Jonas mildly. "Only in so far as I am her friend and adviser on financial matters."

"You and your financial matters. Lagerta is no businesswoman, and that's the difference between the two

135

of you. She follows her heart—she's—she's always been the one to understand my point of view in all this. What are you getting at, you and Great-grandmamma? Do you want me to leave Dondi and the children before I can support them in any way? You both have this notion on the brain. Dondi can't be left, you can't leave a child, and you certainly can't leave three of them. They're all my children, don't you see?"

"They're Dondi's too," said Jonas undisturbed, turning to face him. "Don't whine about them, Gregor, little gold-diggers like their mother. They'll manage very well at somebody else's expense, wherever they end up. And what else do you propose to do? Beg from Lagerta again? You have no integrity, Gregor. You have no integrity any more."

"Have you any," Gregor flared up, "the way you express yourself? This is a shabby, underhand method of attack, Jonas. You get off the real subject all the time so as to insult Dondi. Now I'm going upstairs. If we must, we shall have to manage in our own way, as well as we can, she and I. I expect we'll find a way out. Her nerves are upset just now, but—"

"Dondi's nerves! You think she has nerves?" shouted Jonas. "As a weapon, that's all. She's the coldest, most calculating creature I've ever come across. Just you go up to her, and to Lagerta when she wakes up. But this time I'm afraid Lagerta will have to say she can do nothing."

"I'm not saying another word to you, not another word. You might also remember that during the war Dondi was both clever and courageous. Really splendid."

"Well," said Jonas, "people like Dondi often come out best in disastrous situations."

"As if that was something to upbraid them for. Besides, what do you mean by 'well'? Why 'well'?"

"Well—"

"What have you to say against Dondi's behaviour during the war years?" asked Gregor.

"I could say a good deal."

"What are you trying to insinuate?"

"Nothing. I might possibly enlighten you about one or two things."

"Speak out then, man."

"That can wait, Gregor. There's so much else to think about now. Afterwards we can discuss anything you like."

"What a lot of evasion. And you expected me to accept help from you? To go to Paris! You want to be my benefactor, you with your filthy mouth."

"Gregor, Gregor—"

"There's nothing quite so shabby as insinuation. How can you demean yourself so, Jonas?"

"Which of us is demeaning himself the most, Gregor? You, living year after year on—"

Jonas got no further. Gregor struck him hard in the face and went, slamming the door so that the house shook.

"Gregor!" called Lagerta.

But Gregor was at the top of the stairs already. She heard him shut the door behind him, and was fleetingly relieved that he should have done it reasonably gently. She stood looking up the stairs.

"Are you up again?" said Jonas resignedly behind her. "Is it impossible to get you to rest for a while?"

"Rest!"

"You could at least stay in bed. You'll catch cold after your bath."

"Nonsense, Jonas. Gregor lost his temper, I heard him."

"Yes, he did, he had every reason to lose it. I lost mine. Our nerves are raw in this house, Gregor's most of all. We both forgot ourselves just now. I do wish you'd keep out of this."

"Keep out of it? I was the one he wanted to talk to."

"I've been trying to prevent that ever since he came home this morning. We've had enough of such discussions."

Whereupon Jonas took hold of her, wrapping around her the old dressing-gown she had slung over her shoulders on top of her bathrobe, and tried to propel her forcibly into the room. She refused to budge. Silhouetted darkly against the daylight inside, her chin raised towards the half-light of the hall, she defied Jonas. The scarf she had bound round her head had slipped back, her grey hair hung damply over her forehead and her ears, seeming thin and sparse against her worn face, and Jonas exclaimed angrily: "You look like—like nothing on earth. It's terrible to see you like this."

"Then it'll have to be terrible. You behave as if you had authority over the lot of us. Now let me pass. I *will* go up to Gregor. He looked just as he used to when he was a boy, when something was really wrong. I know exactly how he's feeling."

"Are you going up there?"

"I'll get him to come down, of course."

"In the mood he's in now?"

"Yes."

"What will you say to him?"

"I don't know."

"You'll wake up Dondi, both of you."

"Then let her wake up."

With a sigh Jonas released her, but still tried using

138

reason: "This is foolish, Lagerta. We're not pestering the life out of Gregor you know."

"It wouldn't take much to pester the life out of Gregor at this stage. He's more depressed than either you or Great-grandmamma realize."

"Can't you admit that there are others in this house besides yourself who may be fond of him?"

"Yes, of course. But you two are so high-principled, so severe with yourselves and with everyone else. I'm the only one who's not severe, and who has no reason to be. On the contrary."

"If we were as severe as you make out, things might be looking somewhat different now," replied Jonas peaceably. Lagerta deflated for a moment, but braced herself again. "You see what happens when the two of you get together."

Wearily Jonas turned away from her, looking up at the fanlight over the door as if he might find advice or a solution there. He said nothing, and Lagerta hurried past him up the stairs, incredibly light-footed and quick in her slippers. He heard her knock softly, heard the door open carefully, heard whispers, quiet footsteps. He went outside, sat down on the doorstep and, elbows on knees, buried his face in his hands.

Lagerta had sat down in her usual place by the centre table in the living-room. Gregor remained standing. He stood as if in defiance, and Lagerta dared not make a move at first. When finally she said quietly: "Sit down here for a little, won't you, Gregor?", he slumped down on the nearest chair without looking at her, erect at first, and then with bent back, his hands dangling between his knees. He so resembled himself as a boy—when he would come in wet, for instance, and would be told to change, not only his shoes and socks, but his trousers as well—that Lagerta permitted herself the shadow of a tender, reminiscent little smile. She could almost hear his despairing 'Change my trousers too!' from those days.

There had been only one thing to do, leave him without more discussion. A little later Gregor would come down from the boys' room having changed his trousers, and there the matter would end.

Her hand made a slight, involuntary movement as if to take one of his, but prudently returned to rest in her lap, shy as a mother's hand. If only things could be settled today as they used to be, almost without being mentioned. If only she and Gregor were the only ones involved. But it was no longer just herself and Gregor.

"Did Jonas go?"

"Yes, he went."

"You mustn't think that I'm not aware of all I owe you, Lagerta, that I don't realize we're a burden to you."

"You're no burden, Gregor."

"If only Jonas wouldn't interfere in everything. He's such a busybody. If I could only get some peace and quiet for a little while longer . . . "

"It's just that he thinks you don't get any at all under present conditions."

"Is that your opinion too?"

"I don't really know, Gregor. I . . . "

"Hmm . . . "

Silence.

"You have to be true to something," said Gregor after a while. "You have to achieve something," he said. "It's simple-minded of me, I suppose, but I believed I would. I've gone on believing it."

"I too, Gregor."

"If only I were something else instead of an author. An author isn't a person, he's—he's an anomaly. He doesn't fit into any pattern. I behaved abominably to Jonas just now too."

"That'll right itself. Jonas doesn't bear a grudge for long. And he means well."

"People like him always mean well. Right up to the point where money enters into it. Then they're brought up short."

"He does understand money. The rest of us don't."

"I'm glad I don't owe *him* anything at any rate. I do to a certain extent of course. We live here, we eat here year after year. He's got it all written down, if I know him. The little I earn . . . If there's enough to buy a few clothes and cover expenses of that kind, it's quite an achievement."

"Don't let's discuss that, Gregor. The point is what are we going to do now? The business—"

"Jonas wants to liquidate it. He's always been against the idea, and now he wants to liquidate it. That would mean quite a to-do. You'd lose money on it and—"

"Oh, never mind about me."

"Jonas thinks you can't afford it, that we're cleaning you out, in fact," said Gregor in embarrassment. "But supposing we tried to go on a *little* longer? It might improve. I've had the naïve belief that if only I could finish a proper book I'd—oh, get ourselves equipped, begin to pay off my debt to you and Jonas, get things straightened out."

"You shall, Gregor. Whatever happens, you musn't give up your work."

"Heavens, Lagerta, writing's simply a luxury you know. If there's anything you really need a fortune for, it's for being—I won't say an author, that's no word for me to use, but someone who lives by his pen. A scribbler. I didn't become an author, but I'm condemned to write. I wish I could be of use in some other kind of honest work, but you have to be qualified for the kind of job on which to feed a family. In the old days they had use for someone as simple as a stonebreaker, but not now. Even as far north as this they have machines."

"As long as this matter of the business can be settled, Gregor—"

"Oh yes, the business. It's been a nightmare. If I so much as suggested to Dondi that it might not work, I was interfering and suspicious. I can't understand why it should be so damned urgent all of a sudden."

"It has something to do with bank drafts," said Lagerta, dropping her voice.

"Good God, has Dondi . . . ?"

"Not Dondi, Andersen."

"Andersen? I've never been able to stand that fellow. Has he forged something?"

"Not exactly. Dondi will have to explain it to you herself. I find it so difficult to understand that sort of thing."

"So does she, Lagerta. Nothing could be further from her capacities—But you were both so keen on the idea."

"Yes, and it wasn't a success. But we'll find a solution," declared Lagerta with the courage born of a mother's desperation.

"I can see nothing for it but to go on writing small pieces of muck until the youngsters can fend for themselves, and afterwards too. Besides, when will they ever be able to do that? What's to become of them? Jazz crazy kids . . .

"Everything I do turns out to be a failure," said Gregor. "My life and my work. I'm the sort of person who should have fixed office hours. That's respected, it's understood. But writing—when does a person 'write'? When other people's activities permit it. Someone who isn't tied to specific hours of work ought to be able to adapt himself to his surroundings, whatever next! The narrow edges bordering on the existence and the conflicts of others are for him. Can't he make use of *them*—? I'm not referring to you, Lagerta, you know that. Not to anybody really. That's how life is."

"Dust and ashes, Gregor?"

"Dust and ashes. Dead dust and dead ashes. All of it dead, dead, dead," said Gregor harshly. "Don't try to console me on that score."

But he seemed to regret his harshness. " 'What is he doing now?' " he quoted in a more amenable tone. " 'Is he working on anything, anything important?' They may not be so heartless as to ask you to your face, but you know they're thinking about it all the time. As things are they must be thinking about it. You don't know yourself whether you're working on anything, whether what you're fooling with will prove to be any good. You wait, wait, wait, listen, listen, listen, while time passes and everyone else waits and listens too."

Gregor began to speak quietly and monotonously, as if to himself. It struck Lagerta that he was talking in a trance, talking in tongues, about things he had never mentioned before as far as she could remember, and which deprived him of his will, just as something had deprived her of her will the night before. She felt as if she were listening to some kind of testimony.

"Those dead days," said Gregor. "No-one can know what it's like unless he's attempted it himself. You feel good for nothing, you go back to the everlasting stories again so as to have something to occupy yourself at least, and to earn money for some necessity or other. Then you've raised yet another barrier against something more important, which was trying to work itself to the surface. Your subject-matter—you don't just sit down and write about it. You have to mature towards it, find the thread in it, live with it for a long time before you can find the thread. And leave it repeatedly. And learn all about it afresh when you return. You spend your time rummaging. If people had any idea of how hopeless you can feel after a day of such rummaging. But who understands that, except a few other unfortunate scribblers, perhaps.

"Feeling your way, guessing your way, writing haphazardly, sheer rubbish. Better that than to get nothing on paper. You may find a grain later in the empty talk. Real knowledge comes only in flashes. They strike like lightning and if they're not seized at once they may disappear again for ever. They may turn the whole thing upside down and yet you must thank heaven for them.

"*Waiting*—that's the secret. If honest folk knew how painful that waiting was . . . No, it's an occupation for rich recluses, that's what it is.

"And then all the learning that's considered necessary these days," said Gregor, his voice loud with anger all of a sudden, running both hands through his hair so that it stood up on end. He began walking up and down. "All the things you're supposed to have read if you want to be listened to. Freud, and the devil and all his works. To me it seems as if all that must be more of a hindrance than a help. Such and such is in the textbooks, the action must take place thus and so because the characters have been through this, that and the other, not only since they were born, but *before* they were born. If you don't follow the tune you're behind the times with a vengeance. I have no confidence in it, I can't fathom it. It has an unhealthy, repulsive effect on me; it seems irrational, akin to the rummaging of the ancients in the entrails of sacrificial animals in order to read the future. If it only applied to the sick, but no, it applies to us all. There's even talk of 'healthy neuroses'.

"And then I don't understand symbols either. Nor cutting the text down to the bone so as to make it 'spare'.

I yearn for words, to choose between them. I don't favour a torrent exactly, but I do like a certain abundance and richness. I can't take so much interest in 'form', all I have is my old-fashioned 'realism'—the things I believe I can see . . .

"In any case, nobody takes me into account much any more. A little of the sewing-circle public perhaps, kind, simple-hearted country ladies not yet touched by the waves of fashion, and not subservient to them. One fine day they'll probably be washed away too, it's amazing what fashion waves can do. Then my publisher won't take the risk of advancing me so much as three hundred *kroner* any more.

"Those three hundred *kroner*—the consolation prize when no more is forthcoming 'owing to previous advances'. Then, if not before, you realize you're at the bottom of a piece of machinery you never dreamt was there when you began to write—a mill turning and turning above your head, grinding out regular salaries to a mass of people with permanent appointments. You've been turned into the silkworm on the mulberry leaf with the whole of the silk industry on top of you.

"Those three hundred *kroner*. Perhaps you get fairly good reviews, some praise into the bargain, and the future begins to look a little brighter. Then the three hundred *kroner* arrive, followed by pressure from people who have given you credit, discreet enquiries about your finances—not so discreet that you won't know what they're getting at, of course—friendly advice to be sure to apply for *all* the stipends going. You apply and get one that doesn't affect your position one way or the other. And in the middle of it all the interviewers turn up with notebook and fountain pen wanting to know the 'meaning' of your last book; wanting ecstatic effusions about the happiness of writing, and how you desire nothing more than to be able to go on and on with it . . . The trouble is you know far too much about such happiness, as you sit, nauseated by it all.

"I remember tearing down to the station with some manuscript and getting proofs to take home with me, day after day after day. The telephone kept on ringing to say it would have to be done faster—I suppose they thought I was out walking. It was like feeling the lash, torturing your brain, and feeling the lash once more. The children screamed, Dondi screamed. I can still feel the exhaustion of that experience and I shall never be rid of it."

"Why didn't you say anything, Gregor?" cried Lagerta miserably.

"Say anything? You had just given us that trip to Italy, Jonas had paid out my 'inheritance' for that damned villa. Say anything? There are limits. No, if scribbling isn't a luxury for rich recluses, I don't know what is. They can give a damn for the whole industry and present their finished product when it *is* finished. But I had a wife and children, two children . . . My second 'collection' had to be expanded, it's scope wasn't broad enough. The public prefers so and so many pages, and short stories don't go down well in any case. I expanded it all right, I didn't know what I was writing, I was numb. I didn't want to be a burden to others; now my family is a burden to others year after year. But it's wrong of me to come whining to you when you've been so— so—"

"You've never been a burden to me, Gregor."

"No, you—?" Gregor broke off and looked at Lagerta as if just discovering her. "I always came to you as a matter of course."

"Only once, Gregor."

"Once? My dear, countless times."

146

"I remember only one. You asked me about Dondi. Whether I liked Dondi."

"Oh—? I was thinking about money."

"I offered you that," said Lagerta a little lamely.

"Jonas doesn't think so."

"But of course I did."

"I thought so too. No, where writing's concerned, I know far too well what's involved for someone like me. I tell myself every single day: Don't let yourself be panicked by the hacking up of time into a thousand small pieces, by those incessant little occurrences that bear no relation to your writing—weave it all together again as if—as if it were a piece of knitting. Don't give in to that dread of emptiness, of staleness, of hopelessness—keep on believing that one day you'll find the right thing. Because something *right* exists, Lagerta, something buried deep in the subject-matter, and you have to clear a way to it, word after word, a little at a time. Far, far off there is a moment *waiting*, when you can begin to shape it on broader lines, to 'create' as the people with pens and note-books say—thinking I suppose of something akin to the spirit moving upon the face of the waters. But—before you reach that stage the book has to come out, and for someone like me it *must* come out, for the sake of the money, so that my debt won't grow any larger, so that the world won't collapse, and because the time is ripe. For a thousand and one reasons the time is ripe . . . A mediocre 'author', what is he? A man tensed at his type-writer, never up to date. In debt to his publisher, in debt to you people here for the money put into the house, for the money put into Dondi's shop, for four people's board and lodging year out and year in. What have Andersen's bank drafts got to do with us, anyway?"

"It's rather complicated, Gregor."

"It must be. Dondi didn't say a word about Andersen's

147

bank drafts, but I suppose that sort of thing is beyond her."

Gregor stared perplexedly in front of him, smoothed down his bristling hair and exclaimed suddenly: "And how those people talk!"

"What people, Gregor?"

He was silent for a little, and then spoke quietly as if making a confession: "The people in my book, Lagerta, the people I'm 'working on', if I dare put it like that. The people I'm trying to keep alive parallel with everything else; with whom I struggle at close quarters as best I can when I think I have a little time in front of me; whom I can't get to move from the spot; and who perhaps turned into a mere fixation a long time ago. I didn't get anywhere with them—that was several years ago. So I thought—I thought: Let them talk, let me hear what they're saying, then perhaps—My God, Lagerta, since then they've talked incessantly, talked all day and all night. I ought to be glad when they don't all talk at once, that happens too. Well, so then I began to write down what they said, when I got the chance. Much of it was lost, naturally, things that may well have been decisive, that would really have thrown light on—on the 'plot'. It became one big jumble of dialogue, incredible drudgery just finding out who said what and getting the conversations into fairly reasonable order. It may be a good thing for a dramatist to get his material down in that way, but I'm no dramatist and my characters are anything but dramatic. The more I listen to them, the more it's brought home to me that they're ordinary people of the simplest kind, that they've appeared in literature thousands of times, as minor characters at any rate. They're not mad, not exclusively sexual, not psychopathic. Not especially gifted either; not artists, scholars, politicians; not even a little profound. Conventional people, and the women

148

are not young or beautiful or attractive in any other way. But if these people get hold of someone ready to listen to them, there's no knowing when they'll stop, you can't get rid of them again. They run in and out of my head and pester me with their boring conflicts. You may ask why I bother with them at all? It's they who bother with me. They simply came, and I'm no good at shaking anyone off, I haven't got the knack of it."

"It's not easy either, Gregor. Do sit down for a bit." He sat down. An expectant, almost hopeful expression passed over his face, and was gone again. "If I could get away and mess about by myself for a while . . . There's always so much more in your material than you dreamed possible. But even if one day everything is right for it, then something inside may misfire. It's not laziness, Lagerta. I don't know what it is.

"And now Jonas comes along in the middle of it all and suggests that I leave Dondi," added Gregor, his voice hard again. "In the first place all big changes knock the ground from under one's feet for a long time, but of course he wouldn't understand that. In the second place, it's enough to have one wife on my conscience."

"But Gregor, surely you don't still think of it that way? It was an accident, pure accident."

"Caused by me," said Gregor with a bitter laugh. "None of you would ever admit it. I said so, I said so, but nobody listened to a word, not even the police. I let go of the wheel, Lagerta, I let it go and kissed Harriet. We behaved as if we were in a daze that morning. She kissed me, and I—She didn't know a thing about driving, she had no idea how easily accidents can happen. But I knew better."

Gregor hid his face in his hands. "We had just started out," he said into them. "I *saw* the bend in the road . . . "

Lagerta sat for a moment unable to find her voice.

Then she said: "It was an accident just the same, Gregor."

But Gregor answered with deliberate composure. "Dondi knows about it. I've never been able to bring myself to mention it, but she's strange that way."

"How can she know about it if you've never mentioned it? She wouldn't harp on anything like that, surely?"

"Dondi harps on anything she can get hold of," rapped out Gregor. "You know how impulsive she is," he said, mending his words. "Remarks fly out of her mouth. I expect she regrets it afterwards, but . . . Now Jonas wants me to let her go, but I must try to solve this problem of Dondi, I can't run away from it. And yet I only make her unhappy."

"She certainly isn't happy."

"And it's my fault. I'm not the right man for Dondi. Sometimes I've even thought: If only she'd fall in love with someone else, if only she'd come home one day and it had happened. Someone who suited her better. But no . . .

"I didn't distinguish myself in the least during the war either. I wasn't put in a concentration camp here or in Germany, I wasn't in England, I wasn't even in Sweden."

"My dear Gregor, somebody had to stay behind. After all, the country wasn't completely depopulated. The rest of us didn't distinguish ourselves either. Besides, you were taken as a hostage."

"For five days, at the very end. Perhaps I'm mistaken, but—if something of that kind had happened to me, maybe we'd have recaptured some feeling for each other, Dondi and I. She's so—romantic really. Being parted for a long time, a little danger, not this everlasting, daily friction. She went away now and again of course, but it was never long enough, and it lacked excitement."

"Could we arrange for her to go south for good," said Lagerta tentatively. "She and the children?"

"Good God, arrange something for Dondi! You might as well arrange something for an infant. It still wouldn't be able to manage without someone to turn to. If you knew how often I have to be strict with her, Lagerta, as if she were a wayward little child. If nobody is strict with her she loses control altogether. I don't know why. She hasn't any less common sense than most people, on the contrary. It's true, Lagerta, you just don't know her, any of you. And now there's such enmity here that you'll never get to know her either. I—I can't stand any worse a conscience than I have already," exclaimed Gregor with sudden fury. "So I continue to behave like a scoundrel year after year, for her sake and my own."

"The expressions you use! You've done your best for Dondi. No-one could have had more patience."

"Patience! That's the sort of small change used by someone with a conscience, to buy a little peace of mind. Merely the instinct of self-preservation."

Lagerta started as if at a sudden gust of wind, but said nothing, and Gregor continued: "I *daren't* divorce Dondi, I daren't take that on myself too. But the business, Lagerta—Dondi says she's seeing to something, and that if only there weren't such fearful haste . . . She won't say what it is yet, but can't Jonas have a little patience? He seems possessed. Why shouldn't Andersen look after his bank drafts himself? But I'm worrying you. Why did you ask me to come down? I—"

"I don't really know why, Gregor. It's just that I'm so upset about it all."

"Yes, yes," said Gregor, almost as if he had said, "If that's all, I might as well go."

Lagerta sighed, and groped for words. "Supposing there were no serious upset *for the time being* . . . And

151

supposing you had a few months to yourself and stayed up at the cottage, really stayed there. Do you believe that then you might—?"

"Believe? I believe nothing. I don't even know what I'm 'working on' until I get the whole thing collected and ordered on paper and can begin to hew it as if it were a block of stone, remodel it. I remember that at long last there comes a point when you can see the material as a whole and—yes, almost master it. You feel a kind of triumph—a happy excitement. You have arrived at—at a period of quiet maturation—everything falling into place like a jigsaw puzzle."

There was a new expression on Gregor's face, a new ring to his voice. Lagerta, not daring to look at him, heard it and said firmly: "I swear to you, Gregor, you *shall* experience it again. I must have *some* money left. It's not so very long since I got interest and so on. Jonas is cautious, you know. But he can say what he likes."

But Gregor's expression was already snuffed out. He said wearily: "Listen to me, babbling away. If you want to be certain of not getting anything more down on paper, just talk. The mere mention of work is dangerous. You've sinned against—against God knows what. I know it sounds like sheer nonsense, but—"

"You said nothing, Gregor, nothing. Now you go back to the cottage and stay there for the time being and concentrate on your work and don't bother about the rest of us. Tell Rasmus you won't answer the telephone, not under any circumstances. We'll straighten it all out somehow."

"Do you really mean that, Lagerta?"

"Yes, I do. You're to have peace and quiet as long as you want. You're not to think about anything else."

Gregor said nothing. He squeezed her hand hard—swallowed, and left the room.

On his way out of the house he almost fell over Jonas, still sitting on the steps outside: "Is this where you are? I thought you'd gone back to town?"

"No, I've been sitting out here."

"I—I apologize for what happened just now," said Gregor in a more subdued tone of voice, sitting down beside him. "I behaved abominably."

"Oh, I most certainly behaved abominably too. Did you and Lagerta have your talk? Keep your voice down."

"Lagerta says she'll help us a little while longer, Jonas. Until I get matters straightened out a bit myself."

"I see," said Jonas. "I thought as much."

"I realize I'm drawing heavily on her resources."

"On Lagerta's resources, of course," said Jonas, scorn in his voice.

"It won't be for long Jonas, only a little while, a few months. I have a faint hope, and she's giving me a chance, a reprieve. You can't very well prevent her."

"Circumstances prevent her. We've reached the bottom of the barrel."

"We—?"

"Yes, we. Or I, if you prefer. I can't do anything more for you Gregor."

"What do you mean, *you* can't? It's true we're living here, all four of us, and . . . You've had some bad years since the war, I know that."

"I'm glad you're not dishing up the argument that Dondi is seeing to something, for that's just one of Dondi's thumbscrews. All right, I won't be malicious, but you simply must understand that either we come to a reasonable settlement, or we face complete ruin, if not today, then certainly tomorrow. If you feel optimistic about any work you may be doing, you must find an opportunity to complete it, and you must do so while I can still help

153

you a *little*. It's been some time since Lagerta was capable of it."

"But my dear Jonas, Lagerta—"

"Lagerta is under the illusion that she's been doing it. And I've kept up the illusion as long as I could, for her own sake, and because none of us in this house can ever do enough for her, and because she's like a child where money's concerned, pathetically easy to deceive. Well, it's given her pleasure. Those shares of hers—The interest on them has amounted to practically nothing since the war, and it's not likely to increase for a long time the way the world's looking now. I've kept her bank account going as well as I could. It's been expensive with taxes and all that, but I don't suppose it means any more to you than it does to her."

Gregor was dumbfounded. Then he said, anything but quietly: "And you think you can justify this to Lagerta? Sheer tutelage—"

"Hush! Don't speak so loudly. 'Justify' it to her? If you can justify extortion, then—I'm sorry, that was abominable of me, but I'm tired, Gregor, dog tired. Bad years, did you say? Just now they're very bad. When I was really desperate about everything up here I was often on the point of telling her the truth. But I've said nothing until now."

"It's sheer fraud," said Gregor. "It simply isn't right that she shouldn't—"

"If you so much as give her a hint, I shall take *myself* off, Gregor, and at once. I shall shut up shop and go. And then *you'll* have to see to everything. I'm not making empty threats. You talk of 'measuring' your material, measuring material like a moth. You should have a try at measuring out money on a small scale, an infinitely small scale, so that this infernal situation up here can be kept going. And in any case, what could I tell her? One

154

doesn't say things like that to Lagerta, you must know that yourself. Here come those youngsters again."

There was a clatter on the stairs behind them, the door opened. With a bound Bella and Beppo were down in the garden. They stood there with half-eaten slices of bread in their hands, chewing, looked their father and their uncle over as if trying to decide on the most sensible way of dealing with them, wiped their mouths with the backs of their hands, and took another bite.

"H'lo," said Beppo tersely.

"Good morning. Where are you off to?" said Jonas.

"We want the telephone, but Mommy's in bed, and Auntie Lagerta's in bed today too, we're not to set foot in there Karine says. We've got to go to town now to look for an accordion. If anyone rings, say there'll be a jam session, two o'clock tell them. Here at our place."

"There's not going to be any jam session here today," said Gregor.

"Why not?"

"Because I say so. You'll have to think up something else."

"Something else? Just when we're beginning to get the band into shape and—" Suddenly Bella said: "Is there a big showdown going on then?"

"Yes," said Jonas unexpectedly mildly. "There's a showdown going on. Now you run along. You'll be told later about anything you need to know."

"If there's a showdown we want to be in on it. It's our business too."

"To a certain extent. But we grown-ups must discuss it first."

When the children made no move to go, Gregor thundered: "Beat it!"

They stared at him in astonishment and slunk off,

155

muttering resentfully. Gregor sat down, adopting Jonas's attitude, his face in his hands.

"In all honesty, Gregor, don't you feel sorry for those children of yours?"

"Yes, confound it."

Jonas patted his brother cautiously on the shoulder, got up, and went down the hill to town.

VI

The morning passed in oppressive stillness. The children slunk up and downstairs, banged about in the cellar, were away for hours at a time, then suddenly reappeared, to hang about as if keeping watch, before once more vanishing.

Lunch arrived on the table, conjured up secretly by Karine. Lagerta, who in spite of everything had finally dozed off, sat, dressed, in her usual place; pale, her damp hair only just beginning to curl again. Every time Karine offered her a dish she said absent-mindedly: "Thank you Karine." And when Karine said: "Now Miss Lagerta, you be so good as to eat, poor thing," Lagerta picked at her food, obediently and mechanically.

Out of doors the summer day was as fine and bright as yesterday, with good weather sounds and a light breeze stirring one or other of the window curtains from time to time. Broad rays of sunshine fell into the living-room, luxurious bands of warmth and light, day-clear and ordinary now, without a trace of their night-time unreality. Another of the days of which one dreams in winter-time, as one might dream of paradise. There it lay unused, neglected.

As soon as lunch was over Jonas arrived. "Still quiet upstairs?"

"Very quiet. I hope Gregor can get some sleep too."

"Yes, of course . . . Youngsters out?"

"They were here a short while ago. Karine's waiting with their lunch."

"Don't you bother about them. Let Karine wash up and clear away. They'll probably bamboozle somebody into giving them a meal elsewhere, take my word for it."

"On a day like this, when neither Dondi nor Gregor can bear the sight of them, they're homeless, Jonas. They do feel it, you know."

"All the better if they still can feel something. Those youngsters are aware of a good deal. However things turn out, it'll be no surprise to them. I hope we can avoid having them hanging round here today."

"And what about Great-grandmamma, Jonas? I'm on tenterhooks in case she comes. Such lovely weather, and she wasn't here this morning . . . "

"Let her come," said Jonas calmly.

"Won't it be embarrassing enough as it is? If we could keep her out of it today at least—"

"It'll be embarrassing in any case. We must let matters take their course. A broadside from Great-grandmamma won't do Gregor or Dondi any harm. As for keeping her out of it—! I don't give a damn anyway. Bear up, Lagerta, believe it or not, that's her walking-stick on the steps."

And Great-grandmamma it was. She sat in the chair she usually occupied of an afternoon, knitting. Firmly, from long habit, without looking, she hooked the wool over her finger and gave well-timed twitches to the ball lying on the floor; if it came too close she would give it an equally well-timed little kick, so that it would roll back where she wanted it. As usual she would have nothing, no tea, no coffee. She enquired whether Gregor had come home; remarking "oh indeed!" when told that he had. And she rode her usual hobbyhorses.

"That 'business'," she said. "Poof! 'Getting down to work.' Nice way of getting down to work I must say, lying in bed half the day and driving round in the car the rest of the time. With Kaia. Is that getting down to work? And of course it's coming to grief too, it won't be long now. You all think you can tell me any old tale, don't you . . . Well, today I thought I'd see whether there mightn't be the least little thing I could do to contribute to people's happiness, the people whose company I keep."

Lagerta and Jonas looked at one another furtively. Great-grandmamma went on talking quietly and monotonously, as if conversing with herself. The peaceful little click of her wooden needles filled in the pauses, and there was no need for anyone to answer.

She didn't ask many questions, that was one good thing about her. She listened. "Quiet in the cellar, I notice. Extraordinary."

But sometimes she would pinch her lips together tightly too, and you knew it was over harsh, unspoken comments. A train of ideas about which she had kept silent or muttered under her breath, would suddenly materialize out of the quietness, acquiring a voice and a high degree of reality. It was tiring and somewhat oppressive to have her there, a not unmixed pleasure, but a family has to accustom itself to such things. It has to defend itself as well as it can with quiet manoeuvres, evasive, friendly replies, glances quickly exchanged between its members, subjects quickly changed in moments of danger. At such times it is united in unexpected harmony, unaccustomed accord, and is aware of how transient a state of well-being this is. The danger of

Great-grandmamma flying into a passion was always lurking round the corner.

"Setting hair in curls and bangs on top of a young face that's pretty in any case, is there any art in that?" she now exclaimed out loud. "No there isn't. Anybody could do it. Accounts are another matter," she added, dropping her voice again. "I don't understand them myself."

For a while there was only the sound of the knitting needles. Then she said: "Aren't you going Jonas? You don't usually sit about here at this time of day?"

"I think I'll stay today," said Jonas.

"Hm." The knitting needles again. Then Great-grandmamma almost shouted: "Let them leave each other, and the sooner the better, before they do each other too much harm. Because no good came of it, let me tell you, Lagerta. You were so happy about Dondi that it blinded you. I wasn't blinded, not for more than a couple of days at any rate. Dondi was 'pathetic' you both said! She was certainly dressed for the part. So that she could dupe us innocent folk. Foolish, foolish Gregor."

"Gregor brought out a very good book after Dondi came into his life," said Lagerta irritably.

"Not a bit of it," cried Great-grandmamma. "Do you think anyone could bring out a book because of Dondi? Nobody could, even I understand that much about writing. Gregor's book was finished on the basis of his hope, his hope of at last achieving something he never experienced during his first marriage, because, because—a honeymoon's no marriage. Marriage comes afterwards, let me tell you. He produced a book that had been as good as completed for a long time. All it needed was a little revision. But was it good? We thought so, and one or two critics did, but it didn't sell. It wasn't thanks to Dondi that he brought out that book, it was in spite of Dondi, for there was trouble and commotion from the day they

159

were married. Can you remember anything besides trouble and commotion?"

"I can, Great-grandmamma. I've often said so. And we musn't forget Dondi's home. She had no home. With that mother—"

"No, who could forget Dondi's home? If anything has been dinned into us, it's Dondi's home. Nobody takes the blame for themselves any more, it's all their parents' fault."

"Surely there's something in that?"

"Now and again perhaps. Even lunatics may be right occasionally."

Great-grandmamma resumed her knitting and muttered: "I may not think things out sufficiently, but the way my thoughts go is right enough and nobody will persuade me otherwise. Besides—talking about her home the way Dondi does, thats' what we called disloyalty in my day, and it was considered really sinful. Even Gregor must lose his respect for such a person. And he has too. He'll soon be running off to someone else, poor honourable lad, and getting himself a bad conscience and other inferior feelings," she declared loudly.

Jonas lifted his head warily, but Lagerta interrupted, her voice sharp. "We have no reason to believe such a thing."

"I hope he does," said Great-grandmamma even louder, almost as a challenge. "It would be a step in the right direction."

"We're good at hoping in this house," said Jonas.

"I don't suppose we shall have to much longer," was the curt reply. Jonas looked at her speculatively, as if trying to interpret an oracle. But the oracle closed its mouth and was silent, until it again uttered oracular words frequently heard before: "You say they're not so particular about Saturday night as they used to be? It's precisely in these days that they ought to be particular, the way people rush about. Don't come telling me a man's any different from what he was when I was young. On Saturday night he expects to find the house pleasant and cosy. That's when his wife should create a restful atmosphere, if everything's as it should be; something special for supper, *something* nice at any rate, flowers perhaps—no, he'll bring those with him when he comes home. Because he looks forward to being at home, to contentment at bedtime, to sleeping late next morning. It isn't just the working class either. No, all of us small town and country folk. It's only city people who want to go on the spree."

Saturday night was one of Great-grandmamma's hobbyhorses.

"Just listen to what's going on upstairs," she cried to Lagerta in sudden anger, as if it were Lagerta's fault.

Overhead could be heard quick footsteps going back and forth; chairs being moved and put down again roughly; a sudden, violent argument; wild, uncontrolled weeping.

"It's not Saturday today," said Lagerta.

"No, but it's exactly like this on Saturdays too, particularly on Saturdays. More than once I've felt like tearing down that telephone over there. For that's where all the evil has come from that's preyed on Lagerta's mind. Dondi ill again with one complaint or another; either it was her head, or her back, or the Lord knows what, and everything a mess and a misery up there. Until Monday . . . "

"Perhaps *you* ought to go, Great-grandmamma," said Jonas. "I don't suppose it'll be very pleasant here this evening either."

But Great-grandmamma would not be frightened away. "Thank you, I prefer to stay," she said calmly, and began

161

a new row. And putting her knitting down in her lap she announced: "Besides, I want to talk to Gregor. Alone. Ask him to come down.

"Do as I say Jonas," she continued, for neither Jonas nor Lagerta had moved. They sat curiously still, looking at each other, and made no comment.

Reluctantly Jonas went. Slowly he got up from his chair. Slowly Lagerta disappeared, and Gregor came down. A cold, distant Gregor, who stopped just inside the door and made no move to come closer.

"You wanted to talk to me, Great-grandmamma?"

"I did. We two don't talk to each other very often," she said emphatically.

"Possibly not."

"It's a long time since the last occasion. One never does talk to one's grandchildren of course, not seriously at any rate. One scarcely ever talks to one's children, and never to one's grandchildren. As for one's great-grandchildren —they're like a far-off savage tribe. I've often said so to Lagerta. Sit down, sit down over here, so I can hear you."

Gregor sat down, polite, annoyed, distrait, his thoughts very much elsewhere.

"You sound bitter, Great-grandmamma. Is it anything we've done? Or not done? Have the children misbehaved? If so, of course I'll talk to them," he said at random.

"They haven't misbehaved except by being themselves. Frightful, there's no other word for it. But I'll be brief. One has to be brief with you young things."

"Young things? I'm well on in the thirties, Great-grandmamma, and Dondi—"

"Don't bring Dondi into it. If you and I could speak to each other frankly for once, it might be a good thing. Keeping our thoughts to ourselves only makes us petty. And spiteful . . . "

162

Gregor looked uneasy, but Great-grandmamma continued: "All this is making me spiteful, a spiteful old woman. Old people can change too. It's nonsense to say that only childhood is important. We get spiteful too, and less and less afraid of it. I think really wicked thoughts sometimes, and admit them to myself. I can understand why people commit murder."

"That seems excessive, Great-grandmamma," said Gregor politely, still wrapped up in his own thoughts and indifferent to Great-grandmamma's metamorphoses.

But she said in quite a different tone of voice: "It seems to me you're going through a fine phase, my lad."

"Oh—?" Gregor smiled fleetingly at this remark, not interested in Great-grandmamma's opinions.

"For a long time you had bad luck. To all appearances, I mean. To compensate for it you had certain standards, you never lost your dignity. That's expensive, it can cost a lot of effort."

"And now I've abandoned them?"

"What do you think?"

"Hell no, I have no standards," said Gregor, and more to himself than to Great-grandmamma: "Who can afford standards these days?"

"One ought to be able to afford them."

"That's easy to say."

"Yes, especially for an old woman like me. You don't care what I think. I'm giving you my opinion more for the sake of tidiness than anything else, so as not to have it unsaid. Amongst other things you had standards when you never fell for today's fashionable nonsense, for the belief that people can be classified and their actions calculated according to tables. You didn't take meddling and interference to be insight and knowledge."

"It was only because I didn't understand the new ideas, I didn't believe in them, I was repelled by them.

It was really a fault on my part I suppose, since so many clever people welcomed them with open arms. If that's having standards, I still have them."

But Great-grandmamma went on with her sermon: "Your writing hasn't been at all interesting during the past few years. It reads as if your thoughts had been elsewhere while you wrote. I expect that's how it is too."

"It's not interesting to have to write it either," said Gregor, thoroughly bored with the conversation.

"I don't suppose it is. I've stopped reading your short stories. Well, every time you 'collect' them, of course I look through the copy you so thoughtfully send me."

"Is it worth it?" said Gregor.

"Not really. Frankly speaking, not really."

"It doesn't surprise me."

"That's just as well."

Gregor sat looking at the floor, listening to the sounds of the house, sounds from upstairs, sounds from alongside, and devoting only half his attention to this irrelevant conversation with Great-grandmamma.

Then she said: "I don't suppose you remember, but once I gave Dondi such a pretty dress. I gave her other things too, but that dress was rather special. It was made to measure by Steen and Strøm in Oslo; we sent for patterns, Dondi chose the material and the style, we did our very best. It was a strange kind of ball dress, yes, I think it must have been called a cocktail dress. I hadn't forgotten what it was like to be young. I had enjoyed dressing up in a thin party dress, showing what I had to show, seeing admiration light up in a man's eyes, the desire to —bite me a little, you know . . . But to you young things the memories of an old woman must seem too far distant even to glimpse, like something in Australia or on the moon—and in poor taste too. Besides, they go about now with bare arms and low-cut necklines on every possible occasion, so it can't seem much fun or very special any more."

"Very possible," said Gregor. "I've forgotten the dress."

"I expect you have. And it was wrong of me to offer it to her," said Great-grandmamma firmly. "We had scenes and tears over it as we did over everything else. She had decided for herself how she wanted it, but then she couldn't wear it because she had no fur cape and no proper jewellery and no Italian shoes and no car—it was before you had embarked on that piece of folly."

"She is childish," said Gregor.

"And sly. That dress gave her an opportunity to make a lot of criticisms of conditions up here, and to make a lot of extravagant wishes as if in passing. I ought not to have given Dondi a dress, I ought to have given her some good advice."

"It wouldn't have done any good," said Gregor discouragingly.

"I don't know about that. I didn't give it."

Great-grandmamma fell silent, took up her knitting, made a few stitches and put it down again. "I ought to have advised you to go out on the spree or anything else you had a mind to, my lad. To slam the door behind you and go. And not come home again too soon either."

"That was surprising," said Gregor.

"It's surprising for me to say it too."

"You wanted to talk to me about something," interrupted Gregor, in the hope of steering the conversation in another direction.

"We are talking about it. You need a different woman, Gregor. Yes, now you bother to pay attention. A different woman who would be warm and tender and loving, and who would give you tranquillity. If someone like that were to turn up—but the trouble is, they don't grow on trees."

"And supposing she were to turn up," said Gregor unintentionally, taken off his guard, and bit his lip at once.

"She may be here already, you mean?"

"What are you getting at, Great-grandmamma?"

"All kinds of things. Let me tell you Gregor, if she turns up, if she has turned up, bind her to you. Bind her as fast and as firmly as you can, so that she can't imagine living without you any more. I hope you're still capable of that?" Great-grandmamma added, as if seized by a sudden, alarming suspicion.

Gregor smiled mechanically, as people do smile at old persons and children. "It might not be a question of what I was capable of doing, but of what I had the right to do."

"Every one of us has the right to live," said Great-grandmamma heatedly. "You haven't a life, only a caricature of one. Are you listening to me, Gregor? Dondi isn't the life for you, or for anyone. Dondi is the worst kind of fate a man could be subjected to. That's what you think too, my lad, when you have the courage to be honest with yourself. I'm taking the chance of saying it while I can, then it'll be over and done with. We old people can feel strongly about things too. We've lived a fair time and seen a fair amount; we don't talk complete gibberish, you know. We want our sons to be happy, and our grandsons as well, we want it with all our might. Further than that I can't go. The little savages will have to look after themselves as best they can. Is she at the cottage, Gregor?"

"Sometimes," said Gregor, taken off his guard again, and looking as if he had just been roused from sleep.

"Of course, where else would she be? I shan't ask if she's young. But is she tender and loving? Has she sweetness and *tranquillity*? Does she help you to live?"

"To tell you the truth, Great-grandmamma—"

"Never mind about telling me the truth. You've a lot of lost time to make up. For that you need tranquillity, and tranquillity is one of the most important things two persons can give each other in life. You mustn't waste time, both of you, you mustn't throw away your opportunity. Let me tell you something. If you don't get rid of the first when the second is here, you'll never get rid of her. I've seen that happen so often. You won't have the strength to do it."

"This is a completely new acquaintance Great-grandmamma."

"Not so new that the gossip hasn't started to go the rounds. It doesn't take much in a small place, that's true. But remember that a normal woman in love won't be satisfied with just coming and going at a cottage. If you don't take care she'll disappear again."

"It's not so simple, Great-grandmamma."

"You're not to make it more complicated than it is. Other married couples separate, you see it happening every day, often quite unnecessarily. So shouldn't you do it when it's a matter of life and death? It's a matter of life and death, and not only yours either. You know what I mean."

"Dondi can't be left," said Gregor with finality, and got up. "It's no good talking about it any more Great-grandmamma."

"So that's what you think? Then before you go I'd just like to remind you that nothing becomes any more 'just' or any less painful, or any cheaper by waiting. On the contrary, it becomes dearer, dearer in every way. The day you leave it all to try to become a writer in earnest, I shall help you to the best of my ability with the little I have at my disposal. I wouldn't go so far as to sell my house, of course."

"You talk as though it were a question of going for a

walk, Great-grandmamma. You're proposing a terrible operation."

"Big operations are terrible. They're not undertaken any the less often for that. And when it's a matter of straightforward blood poisoning in a whole family, yourself included—"

"You are wicked, Great-grandmamma."

"Protracted poisoning doesn't encourage good temper. We're all poisoned. We were good-tempered once, fairly good-tempered, ordinary, decent people. We're not so any more. Even Lagerta with her eternal patience is fighting against this poison. As for you—you had talent, or the germ of it. Do you have it any more? Are you even mature? You never had the tranquillity in which to mature, to reach any understanding of yourself. The only comfort is you're not dead. As long as there's life there's hope, they say. If there's any truth in it of course."

"Dondi and I can be happy together sometimes," said Gregor.

"So can all married couples. They get tired of quarrelling, they need a short truce now and again. You're a bungler Gregor, it would serve you right if your girl turned her back on you and went. I don't know what's going on here today. Nobody tells 'Great-grandmamma' anything of course, 'her feelings must be spared', as it's so charmingly put when it's more convenient to keep people in the dark. Do you know what it means to be old, my lad? No, how should you? Amongst other things it means being kept in the dark as much as possible, by your family and by your friends, so-called. I say so-called because nobody's really fond of old people. They're 'sorry' for them, and that's quite another matter. No-one is as lonely as an old person, however large the family may be. Well! Something decisive is going on here today. I don't expect anybody to listen to me, but I can't help telling

168

you what life has taught me—that opportunities are there to be taken, that you should operate while the disease is acute, and not let the days start slipping by once more in the old rut."

"What about the children?" said Gregor.

"The children . . . To be the child of two people in love can be bad enough, such children are often neglected. But to be the child of two people perpetually at odds who detest each other—such children are past hope. Like these children here. All right, you can go now Gregor, I've said what I had to say."

Gregor started to leave, then stopped, turned, and seemed to go over to the attack: "Was everything always so perfect between you and—and Grandfather?"

"I'm glad you said 'Grandfather', my lad. I'm sure he'd have declined to be your youngsters' great-grandfather. No-one is to call him that either, defenceless as he is in his grave, not as long as I'm alive. You asked whether everything was so perfect between us. In those days it took a good deal to make it less than perfect, things like drink and infidelity, and your grandfather didn't drink nor was he unfaithful to me. He was a handsome, educated man, we did the best we could for each other as we had promised and contracted to do. Feelings weren't inquired about so much in my day. The person you took a fancy to as a young girl could seldom be considered. Even if nothing else was in the way, he usually hadn't finished his training, or he was a student or something like that. Some people were engaged for eight or ten years, it's true, but more often we were persuaded to be 'reasonable', and take a man in a good position if he presented himself. I respected your grandfather, I looked up to him, I had no reason to leave him, it was empty after he had gone. When the accident happened and we lost your father and your mother, we felt how strongly we were attached to each other. I was fond of my daughter-in-law, Lagerta reminds me of her in many ways."

"Yes, I see—but surely both you and Grandfather must have hankered after something else now and again?"

"Hankered?" said Great-grandmamma, dropping her voice half-scandalized. "One hankers after so much of which one is ignorant. They say it grows less with the years."

"Doesn't it then?"

"You believe so many strange things about us old people. You know so little about us, you know nothing about us. You've never been old yourselves, that's what it is I suppose. Run along now Gregor."

At that moment Gregor caught sight of Jonas sitting quietly on a chair by the door, and following the conversation with a reflective air. "What are you doing there? Can you walk through walls? When did you arrive?"

"A moment ago. Quite normally by way of the door. I'm waiting to talk to you about matters of vital importance. I have to seize the chance while I can."

"A fine way to go about it. Sneaking round like a ghost."

"Perhaps I'm afraid of rousing the sleepers. How is Dondi, incidentally?"

"What do you all expect? She's thoroughly harassed by all this, and hasn't had a good night's sleep for ages. Of course she knows that you—"

"That we—?"

"That none of you in this house appreciates her exactly."

"No, we don't. We never have."

"In that case you've all been acting like hypocrites."

"Hypocrites? For some years, for a good many years we

did all we could to become fond of her. To win her over, if you like. If that's hypocrisy, then—"

"It is hypocrisy."

"Would it have been better if, from the very beginning, we—? That is, if we had not taken pains to—"

"It would have been honest at least."

"Honesty is often the same as lack of consideration. It can make many situations impossible."

"It makes for fresh air. You know where you stand," said Gregor, his face tense.

"What would you have done if we had shown Dondi ill-will from the start?"

Gregor threw back his head. "Taken her with me and left. Protected her from the lot of you."

"Gregor, Gregor, have you gone so far as to lie to yourself as well?"

"I lie to no-one. It's the rest of you who are liars. Except for Lagerta, of course."

"Someone's coming downstairs," said Jonas. He raised his head and listened. They all listened.

"Come in," said Gregor loudly in answer to the knock. The door opened, and there stood Dondi: pale, with dark rings under her eyes, unexpectedly composed and unexpectedly neat, dressed in a high-necked black frock, her flaming red hair combed back smoothly. They looked at her in astonishment.

"Sit down, Dondi," said Jonas cordially.

Dondi took the nearest chair and Gregor went and stood at her side with his hand on its back. He patted her on the shoulder, and Dondi lost her composure. She wrung her hands, her breathing became choked and passionate, her teeth chattered so that they could be heard, and she looked about her, troubled and helpless.

"Where's Lagerta? I wanted to talk to her."

"She'll be here in a moment. We needn't discuss the business immediately, there are a lot of other things to talk about. You're not happy here with us any more, are you Dondi? You're not really happy with Gregor either?"

Jonas spoke evenly and patiently, as if prepared to do so whatever the provocation.

"You interfere to the most incredible extent, Jonas," said Gregor incensed.

"I do so out of necessity. What did you want with us all, Dondi? You had been here before, you knew Gregor and his background when you came so far north to live. You had a home in Oslo, you could have stayed with your mother as you did earlier on."

"With two children?" came pat from Dondi.

"The children could have been provided for. Gregor isn't the sort to run away from his plain duty."

"Gregor!" cried Dondi cuttingly. "I thought I was going to lead a nice life, that's what I thought. I believed in Gregor, I did. He was young and had talent. But what use does he make of his talent? He hasn't even got the sense to know the right people and keep himself in the limelight."

Dondi's voice trembled dangerously. Gregor put his hand on her shoulder: "Let's go upstairs again, Dondi. It was good of you to come down, but you're not yourself, and—"

He tried to get her up from her chair, but Dondi twisted herself free and began to sob. She sat upright, sobbing and looking straight in front of her with her mouth square, like a little child.

Over by the door Lagerta had come in quietly and was sitting with her hands in her lap. They lay there as if to no purpose, palms upward. Her face twisted and became unrecognizable with dislike.

172

Jonas looked at the floor. Great-grandmamma, however, watched the spectacle with cold, almost expectant attention. She had put down her knitting. When Dondi's sobs lessened somewhat, she took it up again and began a new row, as if at a reading and preparing to listen to a long, entertaining passage.

"Look at you all," cried Dondi, her voice hysterical, her words tumbling over each other, the rings darkening round her eyes. "Look at you all. Lagerta, a dried-up old maid, no limit to her virtue, naturally curly hair even, nobody has that any more, but of course she's perfect in every way, all she does is stick her head in a washbowl, dry it and she's finished and just as well too, at least we avoid having her nosing around; Great-grandmamma, who dates from before the Flood; Gregor, so naïve you can hit him with a sledgehammer; and Jonas, who's the one in command, so to speak. A nice commanding officer, I must say, a confirmed bachelor, an ordinary little small-town merchant who can't even find himself a wife, who knows whether he's normal? He quite probably isn't. The merchant aristocracy so-called, a fine aristocracy. We know Lagerta has money in the business, but of course she never mentions it. She's so devilishly refined, so designingly tactful that she keeps everything hanging about in the air rather than have it talked about. God, the assurance in this house, the inevitability, the faultlessness. How I hate it all!"

And Dondi sobbed violently again, while everyone round her was struck dumb. Gregor had a strange expression on his face; he raised his eyebrows, grimaced and shrugged his shoulders as if repudiating all responsibility. He breathed hard, almost as if sighing.

"Well, that's plain speaking for you," managed Jonas finally.

"Come along, Dondi," repeated Gregor. "You don't

know what you're saying. And Jonas, the rôle you play doesn't give you the right to interfere in whatever you please. This conversation isn't fair to Dondi. She's not in a fit state to discuss anything just now, and you're taking advantage of it. It's shabby of you."

But Dondi twisted out of his grasp again, and stayed sobbing in her chair, and Jonas said peaceably: "Surely we can talk about whatever it was Dondi came down for. After all, Lagerta's here now."

Pause. Then Dondi hiccuped: "I've done all I can for the business, sent letters, sent telegrams. I'm waiting for a reply to a telegram now."

Nobody asked who it could be from, and Dondi cried out excitedly: "It's not a matter of life and death I suppose? But where *money's* concerned . . . "

"If we can't discuss this calmly we shall have to give up," said Jonas in despair, and Lagerta added, as if something had snapped inside her, "What *wrong* have we done you, Dondi?"

"That's just what's so terrible," cried Dondi. "You never do anything to me. You're simply not true. You don't even answer back."

"What if we did answer back, what if we started bickering? Would that make things any better?"

"Much better. Then one could get to grips with you. As it is you're doing all you can to hold me down. It's like knocking oneself against a brick wall."

"Hold you down?" said Lagerta in quiet astonishment, as if given something to think about. "Are we so terrible?" she asked. And Jonas said: "You've made yourself very expensive for us, Dondi, whatever you think of our efforts."

Whereupon Dondi howled: "He says I've made myself expensive. Do you hear that, Gregor? Your own brother

174

sits here and says that! And I've made sacrifice after sacrifice, and no-one has realized it."

Puzzled silence. Dondi dried her tears with the back of her hand like a small child and hurried on. "Sacrifice, sacrifice, sacrifice, all the time sacrifice! But the real sacrifice, the great sacrifice—"

Here Dondi broke down with weeping, and when she spoke again she did so in an exhausted little voice, which scarcely resembled her own. "Flowers arrived—a letter arrived too—I gave everything back to the messenger, I didn't dare accept them—I didn't dare look at him on the street—I looked *away*. I knew that the greatest experience of my life was passing me by time after time. Politics had got mixed up in—in the most natural things; those who fell in love with *them* became 'outcasts'. He was a fine man, his name was *von* something. It wasn't his fault he came here. He didn't do any harm either—we never heard that he did any harm. He just *was* here, poor fellow."

"Whatever is Dondi talking about?" said Lagerta, stunned.

But Dondi was already attacking from another angle. "That car," she cried, having found her voice again. "I'm not the slightest bit crazy about it, but now it has to look as if everything has been done for my sake. It was for Gregor, so that he should have 'peace'. For his everlasting scribbling, that gets him nowhere."

Silence again. Jonas said: "Nobody mentioned the car, but you're not entirely mistaken in thinking we did some things for Gregor's sake, in order to protect him from you, and so that you should have something to keep you busy, to occupy you."

Dondi was also struck dumb for an instant. Agreement seemed to be a new and unexpected enemy tactic before which she had to collect herself. She did so and cried:

"Gregor, Gregor all the time! Gregor's books! Old-fashioned and stupid and—"

"So that's what you think of them?"

"It's what a lot of people think of them. It's what all the people who don't buy his books think of them. It's what practically the whole of Norway thinks of them!"

"Do you hear that, Gregor?" said Jonas. Gregor smiled the brief, slightly crooked smile one keeps for habitual trouble, made no reply, but released the back of Dondi's chair. He went and stood at one of the windows and looked out on the evening sunlight.

"Here he is plodding along with those old books of his. Compared with everything modern Gregor's books *are* terribly old-fashioned. Some people must read them, since he still gets his miserable advances, but none of the real critics bother about him any more. Only the small signatures in the minor columns of the newspapers—in small type. And he won't make any effort to keep in with people. There *are* things you can do, not here of course, but all the time we lived in Oslo it was just the same. You can be pleasant and sociable, for instance. When I think of the success he was once! You'd think it would be easy enough for him to do it again. But he has no enterprise, he does so much less than he could."

The words fell from Dondi in an unbroken stream. Gregor turned from the window. "Do we have to bring all this down here?"

"Yes, we do," snarled Dondi. "Talking to you is like talking to . . . a post. I've done it for years without getting anywhere. They're welcome to hear about it all and what I've had to put up with. I've never said anything about it before, but—his publisher, the big one, offered him an annual sum of money on condition that he delivered a novel a year, pledged himself to do it. It wasn't an enormous amount, but it was something *permanent*. Do you think he wanted it? No, he wouldn't be 'tied down'. As if everyone isn't tied, as if I'm not tied with the twins and everything. As if his books couldn't easily be turned into a novel a year with a bit of effort. But I know how much he wastes his time. I caught him once at the cottage. He wasn't sitting writing at all, he was out walking far away on the mountainside. He doesn't stick his notices in a book either, like other writers. He tears them up, laughs and tears them up, even when they're not at all bad. He simply isn't normal about it, believe me. I thought being married to a writer would be like—like—and then it turns out to be thoroughly ordinary, it couldn't be more ordinary. I thought he was such a genius, but as long ago as in Italy I realized he—

"A proper author isn't like that!" cried Dondi. "The rest of them keep up to date, reading Freud and all that. But Gregor is just faithful to the way he began. He's even 'faithful' to his first wife. I daren't mention her name."

"It should hardly be necessary either," put in Jonas dryly.

"Necessary," snorted Dondi. "It's only healthy and right. But you're all so out of touch with things of that sort here."

Her voice sank to a hiss. "The way I've had to degrade myself over and over again to get things the children wanted, reasonable things. I had to flatter, I had to make the most stupid remarks. There's nothing worse for an open nature than to have to pretend. I used to say, 'Go and keep Lagerta company for a bit, Gregor, she'd like that'. If anyone thinks that sort of thing makes people happy, they couldn't be more wrong. Those poor instruments, no-one could imagine what they cost me."

And between tears and laughter Dondi brought out cuttingly: "Just imagine, I wanted to become 'respectable', refined as they say, went to commercial school and everything." Her voice became small and exhausted again. "At home with Mummy we often had fun. She was a good sport. If I hadn't heard so much against her while I was growing up—"

"How about joining forces again?" asked Jonas quickly.

"Thank you, all she has now is one room and the rest is rented out."

"She could rent it out to you."

Dondi, taken aback, was silent for a moment, but she collected herself, found her voice again and remarked with icy dignity: "You can't throw tenants out these days." To which Jonas had no reply. "No, I suppose not," he said, and studied the floor.

But Dondi spoke calmly, as if talking to unruly children. "All of you in this house think you know so much, but you don't know a thing about *life*. Marriage is no joke, let me tell you. Lagerta thinks she knows all about married people's relationships, but someone who's never been married herself . . . She wants 'to have and to hold' Gregor, that's what's the matter with her. She can thank me that he's still got a bit of independence, but nobody thanks me. Everything I do is wrong."

Dondi was overcome by tears, her voice diminished: "I give you up, I give you up. Nothing makes any impression on you. I've tried everything, I don't know how to take you. You might be made of ice and stone. Gregor is just as damnably sensitive as everyone else here, invariably kind: 'But Dondi, my dear, you know very well . . . ' God, what types! Why don't you offer some resistance, seize me by the hair, shake me, throw me around?"

"Like the shoemaker's wife in the chemist's backyard," came dryly and with highly contrasting effect from Jonas.

"I thought we were going to talk about something quite different," said Lagerta in embarrassment, but Jonas replied, "On the contrary. Dondi has attacked the core of the problem."

"This isn't getting us anywhere. Come along Dondi," said Gregor, taking her arm. But Dondi tore herself free and cried: "Getting us anywhere? I wanted to come down and explain myself, and that's what I'm doing for once. I've made allowances as far as I possibly can. This business—it was Lagerta who was so keen on it, she got the licence and everything. It's her responsibility, the way she egged me on. But when it was a question of keeping me here—"

"My dear Dondi," attempted Lagerta in consternation.

"So now, when it's not a success, all the blame is to be put on me. And what about Andersen? He wanted to 'put money in the business' he said. It was his idea to begin paying the bills, not to draw his wages. After all, he was engaged to help me with all that sort of thing. I accept his help in good faith, and he turns on me like this. He could surely wait a little? I've had a terrible time lately, I've worn myself out in that shop. Day and night I've thought of nothing else. But as soon as it's a matter of money I get everyone against me, I know that."

"So you owe money to Andersen?" said Gregor.

"Are you going to be hard on me too, Gregor? It was for your sake I went into the business. I had to do something, after all. Those advances of yours—"

"How much do you owe Andersen?"

"I don't know exactly."

"You should know in round figures."

"Several—several thousand *kroner*. About thirty thousand according to him but he's exaggerating. I'm sure he's exaggerating."

"For heaven's sake, Dondi!"

"It was last year—there were so many bills," sighed Dondi, affecting a woebegone tone of voice. "I hadn't the

179

heart to pester you about them. After all, you had no money. So Andersen suggested—"

"What did he suggest?"

"He had some money, he said. He wanted to put it into something. It was his idea."

"Thirty thousand," said Gregor, as if getting the fact clear.

"Not all at once. We bought new dryers instead of standing with fans as we did before. Fans are right out except in the depths of the country. And new perming equipment, the latest on the market. Things like that are expensive, but if you want to keep up to date . . . then he stopped drawing his wages."

"The man must be out of his mind."

"He is," Dondi assured him, almost revived. "He has the most extraordinary ideas. He tried to rape me not long ago."

Dondi sniffed, paused, and looked around.

Nothing was said. The only person who started a little at the word rape was Lagerta, but she too remained silent.

"Even that doesn't make any impression on you. That he tried to rape me."

"I can't think what would impress us any more," said Jonas, as if to himself. And Gregor said, "You should have told us, Dondi, about that as about everything else."

"Told you? You without an øre to your name? Told Lagerta who hates me, oh yes, she hates me, I knew that long ago. Told Jonas who hates me even more, or Great-grandmamma, who hates me most of all? Whom could *I* tell, whom could *I* confide in? I tried to tell Lagerta this morning, but did she understand? Not a thing. She just got nervous and asked more and more questions. It's a waste of effort to explain such matters to her; Jonas thinks so too, I've heard him say so plenty of times. She

180

doesn't want to know anything about it either. She had hung up before you could count three."

"*Yesterday* morning," corrected Lagerta mechanically, and Dondi said, "Yes, yes."

Gregor was still standing with his back to the room. His voice was colourless. "You must have some documents on this, you and Andersen? Some agreement about back payments?"

"I don't know, Gregor, I don't remember just at the moment. I'm so stupid about money, I don't understand it. That was why I got Andersen."

"He shall have his money," said Gregor in the same colourless tone of voice, talking into the summer evening. "As long as he can prove it belongs to him. He must be answerable for some of the mess he's made, surely? Perhaps I can manage a small payment this autumn if I get out the collection I've planned. Then we shall have to sell off what we can. As long as I can get a bit of peace," he muttered to himself, but his tone was completely lacking in hope.

"The whole point of it was to get you some peace, Gregor, and quiet in which to work. To make you independent of publishers' advances and—"

"Don't mention quiet in which to work."

"Have I thought of anything else all these years? Didn't I come north with you? If you had only tried to pull yourself together . . . "

Gregor shrugged his shoulders. "When does Andersen claim his first payment?" he asked in the same colourless voice.

"One o'clock tomorrow. At the very latest. And he wants—well, most of it at any rate."

This time Gregor laughed. A strange, false-sounding theatrical laugh. "Surely the fellow understands he can't have it?"

"He won't understand anything. I've told him again and again that it's impossible. He just nags about 'drafts falling due' that he has to 'settle', he says."

"But he should have given due warning. Or has he done so?" said Gregor, struck by a sudden suspicion.

"Oh, he's been nagging for a long time. And the lies he's told. I thought it was only his money, and then it turned out it wasn't."

"Don't tell me you didn't even gather that."

"You needn't be so bitter. It was to spare you."

" 'Spare me'—! Come on, Dondi."

But Dondi stayed where she was. She twisted her sodden handkerchief and said quietly, but clearly enough: "Don't you think it's about time to put pressure on the old woman?"

Everyone looked up, shaken and horrified. Everyone except Great-grandmamma. Her expression was inscrutable, it reflected nothing. Had she heard, or hadn't she?

In the silence that followed Dondi said: "What I mean is that she—that Great-grandmamma—would simply be more *comfortable* at the old people's home. And when you think where her house is . . . The site's worth a fortune, everyone says so. She's sitting on a great deal of money."

"Great-grandmamma and her house are no concern of yours. Now you *are* coming along before you say anything more tactless."

Gregor actually got Dondi out of her chair, and had escorted her forcibly almost as far as the door, when it was opened from the other side by Karine, who said to Lagerta in an undertone: "I knocked several times, but . . . It's Kaia from the chemist's, she won't go away. She says she has a telegram for the young madam, and insists on speaking to her too. It's urgent, she says. Should she come in? Is it convenient just now?"

"Convenient, no! Ask her to deliver the telegram and look in later. Another day, say."

But Dondi cried out wildly: "Isn't she going to be allowed to come in even? When she's here with something terribly important, something that may change my whole life, and find you money and—how like you to say she can't come in. My friends aren't good enough for this house, but I have to—"

"Ask her to come in," said Lagerta calmly. Karine disappeared, and Kaia made her entry in narrow black slacks, and loose, hanging shirt; for once something almost approaching perplexity in her thin face with its large, violently red mouth, considered by some to be beautiful and distinctive, by others simply brazen. She greeted the company, looking mystified. "I'm sorry to interrupt. I went upstairs first, but nobody was home."

Kaia was not one to be taken aback for long, however. She gave her long hair a toss and regained her composure. "I have a message for you Dondi—a telegram—you said it was urgent."

"Read it out loud, Kaia," cried Dondi. "You've come just at the right moment. The message is for the whole household."

For a second Kaia seemed confused, almost helpless. She clearly had no idea what to say. "We can't do that, Dondi!"

"Can't?" shouted Dondi. "We're staking everything on one card now, Kaia. It's the trump."

"It's no trump. Look for yourself."

"What?" Dondi snatched the telegram, stood for a moment holding it in both hands, her look of excitement totally snuffed out, then crumpled the piece of paper and flung it away from her.

"You see? I told you so."

"It's your fault, Kaia. You said something stupid in

yours of course, you didn't explain . . . You've ruined everything," said Dondi heavily. "Everything."

"There are limits, Dondi," said Kaia, flaring up. "If anyone's been on your side, I have. I try to help you out of this mess, and then you go and talk to me like that. For years I've provided you with this, that and the other, to put you to sleep, to wake you up again—"

"As if that was such an art," fired Dondi back, "when you have the run of a chemist's shop."

"And have to ask for everything, mind," replied Kaia, equally pat. "There are one or two things I want for myself too."

"You got a new fur coat last winter, you didn't ask for that."

"Sealskin, yes, paid for with medicines. Powders and pills and plaster for two sealers bound for the Arctic. Sewn here in town, and so stiff it can stand up by itself."

"What about that doctor of yours, then?" interrupted Dondi. "He can write prescriptions, can't he?"

"Not in this country, you know that perfectly well. He's not even allowed to practise. If it weren't for the fact that he's so brilliant and knows that as long as he can get over to America—"

"You and your chemist's shop," interrupted Dondi in exasperation. "What problems do you have? You can get away whenever you want, married to an old crock who can't get you pregnant."

"What do you know about it?"

"The whole town knows."

"Everyone has problems, my dear, all real people."

"You don't go round sacrificing yourself at any rate. But I—married to an author whom nobody reads—what haven't I sacrified for my children? If I had so much as *looked* at that man I'd have been called a German whore."

"You were," said Kaia sharply. "There were plenty of people who didn't think you only *looked* at him. And he was an *enemy*, he came here as an *enemy*," she added reprovingly, evidently not for the first time.

"Enemy? As if that sort of thing had anything to do with war and politics. But I had to keep up pretences. I'm not so sure they were right in this country either. We might just as well have been friends with them."

"Not one word more Dondi. I'm a patriot as you know."

"Oh, get along with you, you a patriot? Because that boy-friend of yours left you to go to England? As soon as he'd gone you married the chemist because he got coffee from America. Neither you nor I are patriots, let me tell you. We're just people who've suffered and don't want to suffer any more. I was more of a patriot than you, I rejected the greater happiness."

But Kaia said with dignity: "We wouldn't perform for the Germans, we artists. I made a marriage of convenience. You needn't have had any children either. And twins—! What could be more commonplace than twins. 'Bella and Beppo', in memory of Italy."

"Of a man who loved me," cried Dondi. "You know that very well. As for their names—They nearly got the sort of names everyone else has in this house, Gregor and Lagerta and—I was young and foolish, it's more than twelve years ago. Everyone said it was such fun to have a baby, and then it turned out to be nothing but a lot of bother and responsibility. It wasn't my fault I had two. And you an artist? Kicked your legs a bit in a revue."

"You know nothing about it. A man who loved you? A hotel servant who gaped at you on the stairs. Young, did you say? Oh well, more or less. You're just as *foolish* now as you were then."

Kaia pointed at the telegram lying on the floor.

"Foolish and hopelessly commonplace. Conservative!" she concluded, as if firing a really damaging shot. "Conservative!"

Gregor had stood rooted to the spot. Now he came to life. "Will you be so kind as to leave. All this is of no concern to the rest of us."

"On the contrary," said Jonas. "On the contrary, it's of the greatest interest. I won't deny that that telegram makes me inquisitive."

"Ask Dondi," said Kaia coldly. "I'm having nothing more to do with it. I'll go with pleasure."

At the door she turned to Dondi. "You're in great danger, I've told you so plenty of times, and I have it from a reliable source, as you know. But if I offer you any real help you ruin everything with your everlasting sentimentality. In point of fact you don't care a scrap for those children."

"Was it about the children?" asked Jonas watchfully.

"It was about a journey."

"A journey—?"

"Yes, a journey. Don't go Kaia, don't let them throw you out, you see how things are. Everything happens to me at the wrong time. For once I have the chance to travel properly, and here I am with that revolting shop on my hands. The paltry trips I've taken up to now—"

"I told you, to hell with the right time; you can't possibly set that business to rights, you only make stupid mistakes. Besides, your trips haven't been so bad. You went to Italy, you've been to nice places down south. The last one wasn't up to much, it's true, old fashioned washstands and all that."

"I didn't get anywhere either."

"No, but before that you had opportunities. Once you came home and had met a really fine man, and nothing had happened. That was shocking, Dondi, a fearfully bad

186

sign. Then you get another chance and ruin it with all this nonsense. Klaus should have invited me."

"Klaus? That's a new acquaintance," put in Jonas.

"An old friend of mine," said Kaia.

"Of Dondi's too, it seems?"

"He came ashore from the coast steamer once last year, he and another fellow. We drove round with them a bit, Dondi and I."

"And this year Klaus has invited Dondi to join him on his travels?"

"He's one of the few who earn money in these miserable times."

"A fine fellow evidently?"

"Yes, a fine fellow," broke in Dondi. "Really clever too. Not the type who just goes round dreaming."

"Did you hear that, Gregor?"

But Gregor said sharply: "This is disgraceful. You're all taking advantage of the fact that Dondi's fuddled with medicine and dead tired into the bargain. You know very well, Jonas, she's been taking those powders of hers incessantly."

"She's the only one of us who has had any sleep recently. And aren't they doing research on a so-called truth drug these days? We may have discovered a new one."

"You disgust me."

"Such means are disgusting. But what about this journey? Have you given up the idea?"

"So stupid of her," said Kaia. "A Mediterranean cruise on the *Stella Polaris*."

"With Klaus?"

"Of course. He offered her the trip."

"He must think a great deal of Dondi?"

Kaia smiled a crooked little smile. "He was mad about

Dondi. But she—They talked a lot of nonsense about a long trip, and that if he were to offer her one—"

"And now he's doing so?"

"Not any more." Kaia sighed, rooted in her shoulder bag and found a crumpled, rustling sheet of thin paper with large, business-like writing on it: " 'Tell Dondi *Stella Polaris* leaves Bergen mid-August. Hope she will keep promise and come. Arranging cabin, must have reply quickly if prevented. Cable.' "

"Indeed," said Jonas.

"But Dondi—" Kaia turned towards her aggressively. "First you think it's just a question of sitting in a deck chair and going on expensive shopping expeditions ashore, when obviously it isn't. Then you want him to take the *twins*. I suppose you were going to have them with you on board?"

"But Kaia, we could have sent them somewhere else. After all, he has money."

"Why did you want to bother with them at all?"

"It's easy to say that when you don't have any yourself. If only Gregor was a natural father. But he's an unnatural father, he's not the slightest bit fond of his children. I'm ready to sacrifice anything, and if only Klaus had taken them . . . "

Dondi wept copiously. "I thought he was fond of me."

Kaia shrugged her shoulders, tired of the whole discussion. "To a certain extent, yes. 'Fond of' isn't a very modern expression any more. He's attracted to you, he wants to see what you're like. That's not so strange, surely. And then you tell him you've got twins. If there was one thing you shouldn't have mentioned, that was it. If you had played your cards a little more cleverly you might have coaxed him into that later perhaps, but you wouldn't listen to me. And then to crown it all, you bring that debt of yours into it."

"I won't play my cards cleverly," cried Dondi in a fury. "I can't play my cards. I've tried to play them all my life and I only play them wrong. Why can't I be safe and comfortable and well-off too? I have the right to be, I'm pretty enough."

She wept, the tears streaming down her face. Lagerta remarked quietly, almost with sympathy: "No, you won't try to play them any more . . . " Jonas picked up the telegram which was still lying on the floor: " 'Impossible. Making other arrangements.' Well, that's clear enough." He put it back where he had found it and said with emphasis: "A pity. A great pity."

"What sort of nonsense is this now?" said Gregor wearily.

"I said 'a pity'. For all we know he might have been that man about town I was talking about."

"Be a little charitable, Jonas," said Gregor almost appealingly. He turned to Kaia. "I've thrown you out once before. If you don't go this minute—"

"Yes, you threw me downstairs. I might have broken an arm or a leg, I could have reported you. I'll go with pleasure, I can do no more for Dondi. I warn you once more, Dondi, you're in danger. The only thing that can help you is a new lover, but if I find you one there'll only be trouble. There always is with you. You *should* have been a model with that hair and figure, still thin as a rake though you never slim. You'd have met the right men too. What wouldn't I give for that figure, the way I starve myself. And then you marry an author who had made a success of *one* book! You should have heard Dr. Karik tear his writings to shreds. They have nothing to do with psychology, modern psychology that is. Surely you could have got rid of that awful old man of yours some other way. All right, we know he was rich and that Mummy nagged . . . "

Standing in the doorway Kaia took out a lighter, lit a cigarette, and blew a smoke-ring, looking Dondi up and down: "Get Andersen to re-dye your hair, it's going dark at the roots. Have a perm too while he's around, straight hair doesn't suit you. Stick your stomach out and your bottom in and give yourself a bit of style. And what are you doing wearing a black dress in the middle of summer? A dress!"

"Don't look at me like that, it's mean of you. I hadn't anything else that was black. I can't be bothered to coax Andersen any more."

"No, I expect you've been doing far too much coaxing. I've told you plenty of times, *never flirt beneath you*, girls like us can't afford it. Black! Isn't that like you!"

"What do you mean, flirt? I'm not the stiff and starchy type, it's my nature to be easy-going."

"Poor Andersen, he didn't even get his wages."

"Nobody need be sorry for Andersen, Kaia. He gets his board and lodging for nothing at Mrs. Styrsvold's. 'Handsome Andersen', as she calls him."

Kaia shrugged her shoulders once more. Gregor went up to her threateningly. "*Must* I throw you out again?"

"No, there's no need." Kaia was through the door. She held it ajar, to bring out her parting shot: "You asked me the other day whether it was true that your husband was unfaithful to you? I'll say he is. With the doctor's daughter up at the cottage, if you want to know. She came up from the south this spring, superior type, not at all pleasant. A woman came into the shop yesterday and she said: 'That writer fellow has a lady with him up there.' So now you know, and now the advantage is yours. There are such things as standards. You can demand a certain standard."

"Bravo Gregor," came unexpectedly and firmly from Great-grandmamma. Gregor was at the door in a couple of strides. Kaia slammed it in his face. He stood with it half open, his hand on the handle, while her running feet on the steps and the gravel outside could be heard clearly in the disconcerted silence. Dondi, who had been sitting speechless, her mouth open, rushed to the window: "Is she young? Have you seen her?"

"On the coast steamer once," came the reply from outside. "Young? The kind of face that looks good in any kind of light. I saw her below and on deck. Unpleasant type, as I said, terribly self-assured. According to the latest theory he *killed* his first wife, remember that Dondi."

Quick, running steps again and then silence. Jonas, who was sitting with his hands clasped, rubbed them together thoughtfully. Great-grandmamma folded up her knitting. There was a feeling in the air as of a conference about to be concluded.

"Now then, Gregor," said Jonas. "Shall we say the coast steamer the day after tomorrow? You can rely on me for the time being."

"And on me," said Lagerta, looking at Jonas. Not defiantly, but with determination.

Gregor made no reply. Great-grandmamma said: "The day you go away and try seriously to be a writer, I shall support you as well, my lad. As far as I am able, that is to say."

"Oh, I shall have to try to manage on my own," said Gregor eventually. He stood in the middle of the room, his face exhausted and empty. "If I do go away . . .

"You did far too much a long time ago, Lagerta," he said, rousing himself.

From over by the window Dondi said: "That girlfriend of yours, she comes up there whenever she likes, then?"

"It has happened."

191

"You admit you're unfaithful to me?"

"What you mean by unfaithfulness doesn't enter into it, and as for what does enter into it—you wouldn't understand anyway."

"Bravo, my lad," repeated Great-grandmamma.

"No, I suppose it's so wonderful and out of this world that only the two of you can understand it."

Dondi had sat down again. She twisted her handkerchief, her teeth chattered. Ravaged, coal-black under the eyes, she stared straight in front of her. Then in an icy voice she said: "So you want another dead wife on your conscience? The mother of your children?"

"I don't think there's much danger of that."

Upon which Dondi howled again, the long-drawn out howl of a child: "I am cast among strangers, I have ruined my life, death is all that is left to me!"

"Come along now Dondi."

"Leave me alone! I should never have got that stupid notion of respectability on the brain. Mummy did what she could for me, she gave me a good education and—and —Old Hjerring was nice, he gave me beautiful presents. He might have left me everything. As if what Mummy did mattered so much. Plenty of women do the same nowadays without getting a bad reputation. On the contrary, it's a sign of health, we realize that now. I wish I was as sane about it as Mummy is. It's perfectly all right to let yourself be kept these days too. It was only your kind of life she couldn't teach me."

No-one responded. Dondi stamped on the floor and cried: "Thank God I'm not like all of you, thank God I'm ordinary and ill-bred and common."

And when there was still no response: "Common, common, common."

She wept loudly, heartrendingly, mumbling disconnected words here and there: "To spend my whole life like this—my whole life, my whole life—and nothing will ever happen to me again—nothing, nothing . . . "

All of a sudden she stopped crying. A small, whimpering voice emerged: "What's to become of me if you go away, Gregor? Where shall I go?"

"That will work out all right Dondi. You thought of going away yourself, didn't you?"

"Oh, thought—As if I thought anything. I didn't mean it like that. I only meant—only meant—you know what I'm like, Gregor," she cried out loud. "Impulsive and—thoughtless and— The rest of you are so above everything, you have so much resistance. People who are romantic and—hypersensitive and —"

Again she was overcome by tears, again they ceased. In an altered voice, as if waking up, Dondi said: "Have I been unreasonable again, have I been behaving stupidly? Imagine thinking someone like Klaus would put things to rights for me, a type who just happened to come ashore. I was beside myself, Gregor, you realize that don't you, you know what I'm like. I didn't know what I was doing —Andersen nagged and nagged . . . You know I only want what's best for you, I want you to be a success and —get recognition and —"

"Yes of course, Dondi," said Gregor in the mechanical tone in which he had said it countless times before.

"And that I'm really—fond of Lagerta who has been so kind to me and—of Great-grandmamma and . . . Is it so terrible that I should want to be a little happy too?" she cried again.

"No Dondi," said Lagerta as mechanically as Gregor.

"And I do love you, Gregor," continued Dondi fortissimo. "When I manage to get my thoughts straight, of course it's you I love. Oh, but you've often admitted it."

"Oh Dondi, Dondi."

"Yes, you have."

"Not really," muttered Gregor.

"Were you only pretending then? When you were kind and loving? You don't answer, you don't even answer."

Dondi's voice failed her, but she had managed to seize Gregor's hand and clung to it, dampening it with her tears. His free hand stroked her hair in a weary, accustomed movement.

"I'm your baby, remember," whimpered Dondi. "Your little baby. You've said so lots of times. You've even scolded me.

"You can't deny it," she said triumphantly through her tears. "You've boxed my ears. Boxed my ears, Gregor! Not often, but still—"

"I deny nothing," said Gregor, and succeeded in freeing his hand.

She half raised herself on her chair. "Kiss me," she breathed.

Gregor ceased stroking her hair and turned away. She sank back in her chair and was silent for a little. Then she asked meekly: "Are you going to take her with you?"

"No," said Gregor dully.

"You wouldn't want to hurt me to that extent then?"

"I wouldn't want to hurt her either," said Gregor, still dully. And with a sudden sharpness in his voice he added: "You keep out of this, Dondi."

"Yes, yes," said Dondi, still meek, and wept again quietly. But Jonas called out: "Who's that at the door?"

Quickly he went across and opened it. Bella toppled backwards into the hall, giving Beppo a shove so that he cannoned into the wall, nursed his elbow and gasped, "Damn it!"

"Are you eavesdropping?"

"We've got to. We have our own arrangements to make."

"Your arrangements?"

194

"Sure. And we want to tell you right now that *we're* no problem, in case that's what you're thinking. We've made up our minds already."

Two stubborn, malicious faces, hard and unapproachable. Neither Bella nor Beppo felt affinity with any of them.

There was a pause. Then Beppo said: "We know all about these adolescents' problems, so there. It's in all the papers. They talk about it and write about it. You grown-ups don't have a clue about us, so you shouldn't have the right to boss us about either."

"Get along upstairs, make yourselves scarce," said Jonas.

"That's exactly what we thought we'd do. Go abroad as quick as ever we can."

"We can talk about that when you've finished your schooling."

"Our schooling? We're not going to waste any more time at school. In the first place we'll never be any good at it, and in the second we're going away to be a jazz band."

"The two of you?"

"Us and the Eilertsen boys. A five man band and a vocalist." Beppo pointed at Bella.

"I'm sure you'll go far," said Jonas, ironically but without malice. "Now just you get along upstairs."

"We'll go as far as we want. We'll go on board a collier. You won't be able to search all the colliers. When we're well out to sea, we'll turn out and play for the crew. It'll work fine—"

"And then you'll be put ashore at the first port of call and handed over to the police. Now let's not hear any more of this nonsense."

"Nonsense? Do you think we're so stupid that we'd let ourselves be *put* ashore? We'd go ashore of our own accord, and pick up a car and drive on. That's what all the great kings of jazz did. They ran away from home, by sea or over land, whichever it happened to be. There are cars everywhere."

"You'd steal the car?"

"Of course, we'd have to."

"My children," came in falsetto from Dondi. "I understand you only too well."

"As for you Mommy, we'll come home to fetch you as soon as we get into the big money. My free style, you know Mommy. You're the only person here there's any hope for, for that matter, the only one who's capable of being fun. What if you learned to play something in the rhythm section, triangle or something? You're quite musical, and you like knocking around. Chin up, Mommy."

And Dondi did indeed raise her head, looking in front of her with red eyes as if she glimpsed something there, something unexpected and new.

"Now we must be left in peace," said Jonas with determination. "I'm not going to say it again. We can talk about the future later on. Off with you, at once."

"We'll go, you'll see," cried Bella from the doorway. "All we want to do is jazz, that's what we know about, we've got it in us. Everybody says so."

"Who's everybody?"

"The trumpet and the drums and the accordion and—the whole band in other words. We're not going to fool around with that dumb school any more. Especially if everything's going to pot here. They say in town that you're going bankrupt and all sorts of things. That you're going to get a divorce."

Jonas pushed them both outside, shut the door and turned the key demonstratively in the lock. He took a deep breath as if after a tussle.

Dondi had collapsed in her chair. Limp as a rag, scarcely able to keep her eyes open, she seemed ready to drop to the floor at any minute. In Lagerta's face dislike gave way to a curious expression of reluctant sympathy, something compelling to which she gave in at some cost. She rose painfully, went over to Dondi, tapped her on the shoulder and made her sit up. "Carry her upstairs Gregor, get her to bed. I'll hold the door for you."

She dragged herself across the floor and unlocked the door again.

Gregor had stood motionless. Mechanically, his expression remote, he picked up Dondi and carried her out of the room, while Lagerta sat down again and crumpled completely. Back hunched, head nodding and mouth half open, eyes closed and hands limp in her lap, she lay almost prostrate in her chair.

"Well, well," said Jonas softly, as he stood watching her. And he made a hint of a gesture, something in the direction of fetching a cushion, but gave it up and lit his pipe instead. Softly, so as not to wake Great-grandmamma, who sat nodding, or perhaps only pretending to nod, he said: "We certainly got the whole works this time, old turns and new ones. It's a pity Great-grandmamma looks as if she fell asleep in the middle. A pity—she knows how to appreciate it. The one about death being all that's left is pretty old hat by now, though."

"Jonas!"

"Even Gregor must have had enough of it by this time."

"He'd had enough a long time ago. He'll go away now."

"Unless Dondi talks him round again."

"Not any more. As long as we take responsibility for —the others."

" 'As long as'. We could have had a clean sweep here."

"Clean sweep?" With a prodigious effort Lagerta pulled herself together and sat upright, instinctively swinging her shoulders as if getting an old burden back into place. "That's the kind of thing you can do when you're young. Not when you're getting on in years . . .

"You're so much stronger when you're young," she asserted.

"Yet you obviously think you're still strong enough to take on one meaningless task after another."

"One does what one has to do, Jonas. Anything to do with Gregor will never be meaningless to me. Nor to you, let me tell you."

Jonas did not reply. He paced the floor, puffing angrily at his pipe.

"If we want to get Gregor away," began Lagerta—

"Yes, confound it," broke in Jonas.

"As long as I can be more forbearing, Jonas. As long as I don't worry so much about everything, don't let my mind get poisoned, don't get upset about having to say one thing and think something different—then I shall manage it. Then no-one will need to knock their heads against brick walls either . . . "

"Lack of forbearance is one of your big failings, Lagerta. Forbearance is one of the qualities we need to cultivate in this house."

"Don't be sarcastic, Jonas."

"I'm not being sarcastic. I'm profoundly serious."

And Jonas suddenly brought his fist down on the table so that the objects on it danced, gritted his teeth, and said bitterly: "By God, if he were not my brother—" He stood panting, red in the face.

Pause.

"But he *is* your brother," said Lagerta gently. Jonas rubbed his aching hand, looking ashamed of himself, and she had the courage to say: "You ought to be sorry for someone who can't make anyone really fond of her, sorry for an adult who has nothing but childish weapons to fight with."

"Childish!" said Jonas, losing his temper again. "She's cunning as the devil, do you call that childish? I can't remember Dondi's weapons ever being anything but effective all these years. With their help she's been top dog in this house year after year. And she'll continue to be so as long as she lives. We can whistle for our man about town."

"She's beaten now."

"Dondi beaten? No fear. The rest of us are though. Or do you feel triumphant?"

"If Gregor goes, I shall."

"Yes, yes, it will be something," said Jonas wearily. "But I fail to see why I should be sorry for her. There are plenty of people to be sorry for, and I'm not going to give priority to the most unreasonable. Why should they be allowed to disrupt everything around them unpunished? Let them look after themselves, then they might learn something from it."

"Do you think she should have gone on the stage, Jonas?" Lagerta was astonished at her own words, and Jonas, who had been pacing the floor again, was brought up short: "Dondi on the stage?"

"Yes, you and Great-grandmamma always say she acts so well and has such a large repertoire."

"Her own repertoire, yes. But could she learn a part, creep into another person's skin? No, I can't see her doing it. She's never tried harping on that either."

"There was some reference to her being a model," said Lagerta, passing her hand over her forehead.

"But that's altogether different."

"I only meant, a person doesn't necessarily know herself." Lagerta looked thoughtful, and Jonas looked thoughtfully at her. Then he said hurriedly: "And those youngsters? What are we going to do with them? One fine day they really will run away and we shall have to send the police after them."

"You'll see, when we've got them through school—"

"Through school? With Gregor gone? Not that he's much help, but—"

"No," came unexpectedly and very loudly from Great-grandmamma, who suddenly sat bolt upright in her chair. Lagerta and Jonas looked at her absently without replying, and she leaned back again, as if overpowered and out of the running.

According to his habit Jonas went over to one of the windows, and stood there for a while looking out. Over in the mountains to the west a compact little swirl of mist lay pinned between two peaks. "Here comes the bad weather," he said in a normal tone of voice. "Might have expected it. It'll be drizzling and cold tomorrow.

"Now we must all get some rest," he said, turning round. "We shall have our hands full during the next few days. We may know little else about the future, but that's a certainty at least. I'll drive Great-grandmamma home. I'll go and get the car out."

He went out and came back, leaned over Great-grand-mamma and helped her out of her chair. A bewildered little Great-grandmamma, dazed and unsteady, who didn't even grumble, merely shook her head, exhausted and confused.

VII

They seldom talk about it, but Lagerta sometimes says: "I had a feeling for some time that something was going to happen."

And Great-grandmamma, now well beyond her three score years and ten, very tiny, without colour and without weight, notices perhaps that Lagerta said something and wants to know what it was.

Lagerta leans forward patiently and repeats what she said very loudly, and Great-grandmamma exclaims: "Who didn't have a feeling that something was going to happen?"

And then she is generally off again for a while.

Perhaps Lagerta raises her head and listens to the restless footsteps above, the moody piano playing, abruptly begun and equally abruptly ended. If Jonas is there he listens too, but makes no comment. He shrugs his shoulders, shifts his pipe from one corner of his mouth to the other, goes over to the window.

"Going to snow again," he may say. Or: "It's brightening up." Or: "Looks as if it's going to stay fine." Or: "There'll be no summer this year."

Once in a while he will say: "It's a blessing we're rid of that music in the cellar at any rate."

"And that we got them through school, Jonas."

"That *you* got them through school. I shan't forget the time we had until they were fifteen. Fights and scenes every day, and you playing the school teacher down here, cramming their homework into them word for word. You had to lock the door and hide the key. My word, but you were tired sometimes, Lagerta."

"But you were the one who got them into the dining-room day after day. Sometimes you had to fetch them from right across town. And we didn't have the car any more either."

"But I was able to give them each a box on the ear if needs be. I can't deny it had its satisfaction. And it certainly did them no harm. There was no running away."

"They respected you."

" 'Respect'!" says Jonas in inverted commas to the air outside the window. "They were afraid of me, because I was still a bit stronger than they were, and dared to strike them."

And if a letter has arrived that day, one of the not very happy missives from some small Mediterranean town, or one of the curious, half English letters from places in America no-one has ever heard of—letters which have first been upstairs, and which are brought down afterwards by Karine with obvious disapproval and demonstratively heavy tread, and which begin: "Hello Mommy, how are you, we are fine"—Jonas will perhaps say: "They seem to manage, goodness knows how."

At very long intervals he may remark: "It's some time since Gregor mentioned that book of his. Last year he wrote that he definitely thought this year . . . Travel articles and short stories may be all well and good, but . . . "

"I expect it'll take time for him to collect himself."

Once Jonas asked: "Is he still alone, do you think?"

"I'm afraid so," said Lagerta.

Cora Sandel
Alberta and Jacob
Alberta and Freedom
Alberta Alone

Translated by Elizabeth Rokkan
Introductions by Solveig Nellinge

Cora Sandel's brilliant trilogy traces the painful growing to maturity of a woman and an artist. Born in Norway in the late nineteenth century, Alberta craves knowledge and escape from the shabby gentility of her provincial home. The second novel finds her in the Bohemian fringes of Paris, after the death of her parents, facing the conflicts between loyalties to women friends and demanding male lovers, between the prospect of motherhood and her need for autonomy. And in the final novel, *Alberta Alone*, she returns eventually to Norway, to write seriously, both to fulfil her creative ambitions and to support herself and her son, Tot.

'As though one of the Brontës had written a realistic day-to-day account of life' *Times Literary Supplement*

'A masterpiece ... it reads magnificently well. On all levels, it is a pleasure to read' *Observer*

Fiction £2.50
0 7043 3858 0
3859 9
3860 2

Cora Sandel
Krane's Café

'There's a lot to be heard before your ears drop off . . .'

Krane's Café is Cora Sandel's delicately wicked account of the
scandal caused in a small town in Norway after the First World
War, when one woman declines to do what is expected of her.

Katinka Stordal is the community's finest dressmaker, and the
wives of the town are depending on her to make their gowns for
the coming ball. But she sits in Krane's café with her head in her
hands — defeated by loneliness, the threat of eviction, the
continuing demands of her grown children. Her idleness is cause
enough for public anxiety; but when she allows Bowler Hat to buy
her first one drink and then another, the whole community is
alarmed . . .

Fiction   £3.50
07043 3940 4